NEW YORK REVIEW BOOKS
CLASSICS

THE PROFESSOR AND THE SIREN

GIUSEPPE TOMASI DI LAMPEDUSA (1896–1957) was a Sicilian nobleman, the Duke of Palma, and the last Prince of Lampedusa. He was born in Palermo to an aristocratic family whose fortunes began to decline in the 1800s with the passage of laws breaking up large Sicilian estates. Lampedusa served as an Italian artillery officer during World War I and was captured by the Austrians and held briefly in a prison camp in Hungary. He remained in the Italian military until 1921 and spent the interwar years traveling through Europe and attempting to restore the family estate. During World War II, the Tomasi palace in Palermo was bombed and looted by Allied troops. In the last two years of his life, Lampedusa began writing and produced his great historical novel *Il Gattopardo* (*The Leopard*), as well as several short literary works, none of which were published during his lifetime. Two years after Lampedusa's death, *The Leopard* won the Strega Prize and became a worldwide best seller.

STEPHEN TWILLEY is the managing editor of *Public Culture* and *Public Books*. His translations from the Italian include Francesco Pacifico's *The Story of My Purity* and Marina Mander's *The First True Lie*.

MARINA WARNER's studies of religion, mythology, and fairy tales include *Alone of All Her Sex: The Myth and the Cult of the Virgin Mary*, *From the Beast to the Blonde*, and *No Go the Bogeyman*. In 2013 she co-edited *Scheherazade's Children: Global Encounters with the Arabian Nights*. A Fellow of the British Academy, she is also a professor in the Department of Literature, Film, and Theatre Studies at the University of Essex.

THE PROFESSOR AND THE SIREN

GIUSEPPE TOMASI DI LAMPEDUSA

Translated from the Italian by

STEPHEN TWILLEY

Introduction by

MARINA WARNER

NEW YORK REVIEW BOOKS

New York

THIS IS A NEW YORK REVIEW BOOK
PUBLISHED BY THE NEW YORK REVIEW OF BOOKS
435 Hudson Street, New York, NY 10014
www.nyrb.com

The stories in this volume were originally published in Italian in the volume *I racconti*, published in June 1961 by Giangiacomo Feltrinelli Editore, Milan.

Library of Congress Cataloging-in-Publication Data
Tomasi di Lampedusa, Giuseppe, 1896–1957, author.
[Short stories. Selections. English]
The Professor and the Siren / Giuseppe Tomasi Di Lampedusa ; translated by Stephen Twilley ; introduction by Marina Warner.
pages cm. — (New York Review Books Classics)
ISBN 978-1-59017-719-8 (paperback)
I. Twilley, Stephen, translator. II. Title.
PQ4843.O53A2 2014
853'.914—dc23
2013050864

ISBN 978-1-59017-719-8
Available as an electronic book; ISBN 978-1-59017-742-6

Printed in the United States of America on acid-free paper.
10 9 8 7 6 5 4 3 2

CONTENTS

INTRODUCTION

By the side of the path around the circular, volcanic crater of Lake Pergusa, near the town of Enna in the center of Sicily, a carved stone marks the spot where Proserpina, the goddess of the spring, was seized and carried off by Pluto into the underworld. "*Qui, in questo luogo,*" proclaims the inscription. "*Proserpina fù rapita.*" This is the very place:

> ...that fair field
> Of Enna, where Proserpin gath'ring flow'rs
> Herself a fairer Flow'r by gloomy Dis
> Was gather'd, which cost Ceres all that pain
> To seek her through the world.
>
> (Milton, *Paradise Lost*, IV)

I was giving a lecture in Palermo in 2011 and asked to see the entrance to Hades. My hosts from the university kindly drove me; it was early summer, the lush undergrowth was starred with flowers, and the tapestry of orchids, campion, arum, acanthus, clover, wild hyacinth, thyme, and marjoram was still green tender and damp. Next to the monument I found another sign, which pointed beyond the chain-link fence toward "the cave from which the god issued forth in his chariot." Again, the use of the past historic declared the event's definite reality. In a tangle of bushes and fruit trees, some rocks were visible, but the mouth opening on the infernal regions now stands in private grounds.

Ovid tells us, in his *Metamorphoses*, that the young girls who were gathering flowers with Proserpina that fatal day were turned into the Sirens—the bird-bodied golden-feathered singers with female faces of the Homeric tradition—and then went wandering about over land and sea, crying out in search of their vanished playmate. In "The Professor and the Siren," Giuseppe Tomasi, Prince of Lampedusa, picks up these echoes when he evokes a passionate love affair unfolding by the sea in the ferocious heat of the dog days in 1887. However, in this late story, which was written in January 1957, a few months before his death, Lampedusa gives his immortal heroine the body of a fish from the waist down; in this he is following the more familiar northern folklore tradition of fish-tailed mermaids; of Mélusine, seal women or selkies; and of water spirits, called undines by the alchemist and philosopher Paracelsus. But both species share the special charm of an irresistible voice. In the case of Lampedusa's mermaid, hers is "a bit guttural, husky, resounding with countless harmonics; behind the words could be discerned the sluggish undertow of summer seas, the whisper of receding beach foam, the wind passing over lunar tides. The song of the Sirens... does not exist; the music that cannot be escaped is their voice alone."

"The Professor and the Siren" is the only instance

of fantastic fiction in Lampedusa's scanty oeuvre, but enigmatic and brief as it is, it condenses many elements from both local and more distant folklore into a deeply strange, sometimes disturbing fable; in the manner of Giovanni Boccaccio and of *The Thousand and One Nights*, the tale encloses a visionary and magical adventure inside a naturalistic, quotidian frame story. In the outer frame, Paolo Corbera, a young journalist living a bit on the wild side, who comes from the same aristocratic Sicilian family—the Salina—as Don Fabrizio, the hero of Lampedusa's novel *The Leopard*, meets an aged fellow countryman in a dingy café in Turin in 1938. He discovers the old man is a renowned classicist and senator, Rosario La Ciura, a waspish misanthrope who is contemptuous of everything and everyone around him in the modern world. But the younger man is attracted by a quality of mystery and yearning beneath the spiky persona and grows attached to him; the feeling is mutual, though La Ciura does not let up on his withering remarks, bitter denunciations of contemporary society, and mockery of the imagined squalor of his young friend's promiscuous adventures. Then one evening over dinner at his house, on the eve of a sea voyage to a conference in Lisbon, La Ciura confides in Paolo the story of his first and only experience of love.

In that torrid summer of 1887, La Ciura tells Paolo, he retreated to a shack by the sea on the magnificent wild shore on the eastern side of Sicily, near the port of Augusta. One day, while he lay studying in a gently rocking boat in order to escape the ferocious heat on land, he felt the craft dip: "I turned and saw her: The smooth face of a sixteen-year-old emerged from the sea; two small hands gripped the gunwale. The adolescent smiled, a slight displacement of her pale lips that revealed small, sharp white teeth, like dogs'." He pulls her into the boat and sees her lower body: "She was a Siren."

A recording exists of Lampedusa reading the story, and at this moment on the tape, his rapid, witty rendering comes to a pause with a slight intake of breath, a sigh that reveals the author's awe before the intense presence of his own creation.

The Siren announces herself: She is "Lighea, daughter of Calliope," a name that lays a clue to the story's deeper meaning, for Calliope is the Muse of epic poetry who, in the *Metamorphoses*, tells the story of Proserpina, her abduction, and the transformation of her handmaidens. Through this account of her daughter's irruption into La Ciura's life, the overwhelming epiphany he undergoes through her love, and its lifelong aftershock, Lampedusa is placing himself as the heir of an imaginative literary legacy running back to the pagan past, when Christian repression and hypocrisy did not exercise their hold but instead life was bathed in a luminous intensity and heightened by guilt-free passion.

While the name Lighea (the original title of the story in Italian) echoes the heroine of Edgar Allan Poe's early tale of erotic haunting "Ligeia," the coincidence is not altogether helpful; La Ciura has remained spellbound all his life by his youthful love, but Lampedusa's story does not raise uncanny specters or relish sickly memories. The Sicilian is writing against the morbid obsession of Poe; the passion at the core of his modern mythology conjures the possibility of an earthy, pastoral ecstasy, much closer to Dionysian erotica and its legacy (Mallarmé's "L'Après-midi d'un faune") than to creepy high Gothic; animality recurs in the tale as an ideal. In a startling passage, La Ciura even compares the bliss he experienced with his mermaid to Sicilian goatherds coupling with their animals.

Il Gattopardo (*The Leopard*), Lampedusa's only novel, a Stendhalian historical reconstruction of Sicilian society in the tumult of the Garibaldian revolution, is one of those books that has such vivid energy of imagination it has replaced Sicilian reality in the minds of thousands. The book unfurls a fabric of luxuriantly worked detail, as encrusted and sumptuous as one of the island's embroidered mantles of the Madonna, and its worldwide success with readers arose partly from this sensuous plenitude: Lampedusa piles on pleasurable, heady effects, as in the celebrated ball scene when he parades profiteroles, succulent Babas, and irresistible "Virgins' cakes." "The Professor and the Siren" likewise stimulates each of the senses—we are invited to smell and taste the siren, not just to see or touch her. The erotic avidity of the eminent, scornful professor startles his young friend, Paolo, just as it can take the reader by surprise, too. The old man wants to eat sea urchins:

> "...they are the most beautiful thing you have down there, bloody and cartilaginous, the very image of the female sex, fragrant with salt and seaweed. Typhus, typhus! They're dangerous as all gifts from the sea are; the sea offers death as well as immortality. In Syracuse I demanded that Orsi order them immediately. What flavor! How divine in appearance! My most beautiful memory of the last fifty years!"
>
> I was confused and fascinated: a man of such stature indulging in almost obscene metaphors, displaying an infantile appetite for the altogether mediocre pleasure of eating sea urchins!

Later, Paolo brings La Ciura some very fresh ones for supper and watches him eat them:

> The urchins, split in half, revealed their wounded, blood-red, strangely compartmentalized flesh. I'd never paid attention before now, but after the senator's bizarre comparisons they really did seem like cross sections of who knows what delicate female organs. He consumed them avidly but without cheer, with a meditative, almost sorrowful air.

The effect is a bit queasy, a collision of refinement with explicit fleshly delights. Earlier, La Ciura has quoted the opening line of Shakespeare's Sonnet 119: "What potions have I drunk of Siren tears?"

At this point in the recording, after Lampedusa has delivered the line in exquisitely articulated English, he sounds so moved that he can hardly recover himself to continue. The original sonnet, however, continues in a dark Jacobean spirit, that these tears have been "Distilled from limbecks foul as hell within." The reader may not carry libraries in his head like the author, but turning back to Shakespeare will find that the poet, overborne by "this madding fever" of his love, cries out against the clash between beauty and ugliness, desire and repulsion. La Ciura, idealizing a memory of bliss with one exceptional lover, while furiously denouncing all other women as sluts or worse, recalls Lear who in his madness rains down curses on women's organs: "Down from the waist they are Centaurs, / Though women all above; / But to the girdle do the gods inherit, / Beneath is all the fiends': there's hell, there's darkness, / There is the sulphurous pit, burning, scalding, / Stench, consumption. Fie, fie, fie! pah, pah!" (*King Lear*, IV, 6)

In Shakespeare's imagination, the centaurs that Lear excoriates are—like mermaids, monsters, mythic hybrids of animal and human parts—close to nature and its bounty and violence, and brimful of classical associations with untamed passions. But La Ciura is taking issue with this dichotomy and its freight of sin and disgust. He declares, "I told you before, Corbera: She was a beast and at the same time an Immortal, and it's a shame that we cannot continuously express this synthesis in speaking, the way she does, with absolute simplicity, in her own body."

Lighea's marvelous duality is reflected throughout the story. The old man and his young friend—the one celibate, the other libidinous—dramatize the traditional Greek antimony between reason and desire, the civilized and the wild. Yet, as with the mermaid's form, Lampedusa aims to fashion a *coincidentia oppositorum* at many levels—supernatural and natural, unreal and material, monstrosity and beauty, animal and human, ideal love and lubricious delight—arraying his love story in language that's enriched by his famously wide reading across the spectrum of genres, including Calliope's sphere, epic poetry: The imagery of his siren's peculiar anatomy owes something to Keats's Lamia, as well as to Homer's Scylla. With judicious wit, Lampedusa corrects misapprehensions among his forebears; for example, in canto XIX of *Purgatorio*, a passage familiar to Italian readers, Dante describes a dream of an ambiguous siren, beautiful and grotesque, and remembers how he woke sharply at the stench from her exposed belly. This is the sort of puritanical horror that Lampedusa rejects utterly. When La Ciura evokes the delicious aroma of his siren, he is pointedly redressing the wrong done to the species. Above all, La Ciura's heroine declares, "Don't believe the stories about us. We don't kill anyone, we only love."

The story conveys far more than a sultry passion of summer days long ago; it has radiated throughout the aged professor's life as an ideal of transcendent unity, body and soul, carnal and spiritual knowledge, and he passes it on to his young confidant to initiate him, too, into a pagan mystery about a form of passion to which modernity—and Christianity—has blocked access. With his sun-drenched, aromatic summons of an erotic idyll with a beast who was also a goddess, La Ciura—and his creator, Lampedusa—expresses a dreamed healing of these long, deep conflicts. The frequent references to Hades in relation to the Turin bar where Paolo first meets La Ciura strike the reader as jocular at first, but after hearing the story of his dazzling encounter with the divine, the darkness takes on a powerful metaphorical charge. With the closing pages of his story, when the professor keeps his tryst with the siren, Lampedusa folds together Eros and Thanatos to reach a consummation of surprising serenity. In this way, the author defends mermaids against centuries of fairy lore that warns against their malignant and fatal love.

The figure of the rather feckless narrator reflects the young Lampedusa himself, who attended—rather briefly —the university in Turin, and also stayed with friends in the city for longer periods in the early part of the century. Turin was a center of political discussion and, eventually, of strong resistance to Fascism, and readers of Lampedusa's story take La Ciura's ferocious contempt for the tawdriness of the modern world as an attack on the Mussolini regime: a great scholar denouncing the denatured uses of the classics by the architects and artists serving Fascist propaganda. Lampedusa had felt admiration for Mussolini in the early years of the dictatorship (his sympathies were not unusual among intellectuals in Italy, including his fellow countryman Pirandello), but in 1938, the year in which he set "The Professor and the Siren," the new "racial laws" were passed, and Lampedusa and his wife decisively parted company with the regime.

The figure of La Ciura, however, represents radical independence from the claims of the present—his aloofness and misanthropy exclude any direct political engagement one way or another. He originates in some fascinating compatriots of Lampedusa, whose stories continue the writer's excavations into his island. For example, La Ciura was partly influenced by the scholar Giulio Emanuele Rizzo, a classical archaeologist, born in Syracuse, who published a study of the Villa of the Mysteries at Pompeii, the most sumptuous and enigmatic sequence of erotic paintings surviving from ancient Rome. More significant still, however, is that La Ciura's disappearance at the end of the story was directly inspired by another eminent Sicilian, Ettore Majorana, a particle physicist and mathematician of lasting influence, who was born in Catania in 1906 and vanished on a sea voyage from Palermo to Naples in 1938. The circumstances have remained a mystery, but there were reported sightings in Argentina of someone who looked very like him. For Lampedusa, the likely political reasons, the detective-story elements, and the particular troubled psychology of Majorana are all set aside, or rather transmuted—exalted—into a mythic passage into the transcendent: first experienced as love, like Odysseus's sojourn with

Callisto, and then as katabasis, descending to the depths to be reunited with his siren who promised long ago she would always be there to receive him.

Through the scathing fury of La Ciura and his hankering for the past and for his fairy love, Lampedusa presents an allegory of his passion for Sicily; the mermaid embodies the island's deep time and her spell the ecstasy and the wound that its mad beauty inflicts, and even her materiality conveys the burden of its antiquity, its long history. In his distaste, his hauteur and cynicism, the cynical, angry old man resembles Don Fabrizio, the Prince of Salina and the hero of *The Leopard*. But even more than the imposing, tall, powerful, agile prince, the complex character of La Ciura conveys Lampedusa himself: reclusive, bookish, and determinedly out of sorts with the times.

Yet the "professor" is also rather different from both the fictive Prince of Salina and the real-life Prince of Lampedusa: The once handsome student isn't a decadent aristocrat mired in the stagnant idleness engulfing an entire society but a productive, hardworking, world-renowned scholar who has risen from obscure social rank; his universe is larger than the enervated and stifling island society that the other two stories in this volume depict. Furthermore, as the often startling sensuality of the story makes clear, La Ciura has strong appetites and is able to remember an experience that lifts him out of the general depressive tenor of Lampedusa's world.

The unusual departure for Lampedusa into mythic

territory reveals the versatility of a passionate reader and book-lover who had not yet settled into one mode or decided his genre. But he had found his theme, whatever kind of story he chose to write, and that was Sicily, its history, customs, landscapes, and people.

The manuscript of *The Leopard* was almost lost but finally assembled from scattered pieces, and the work was acclaimed a masterpiece as soon as it saw the light of day in 1958—but by then its author was dead at sixty. The manuscript of "Lighea" has not been traced; the story exists only in a typed copy. In his own eyes, Lampedusa died unpublished, a dilettante and a failure, just one of the many absurd and immobilized aristocrats he satirized, as in "The Blind Kittens"; yet this odd stroke of fate in his peculiar history sharpens the melancholy power of his slender oeuvre. "The Professor and the Siren," the last thing he wrote, feels even more autobiographical once the reader knows that Lampedusa was about to die when he was writing it.

The two other stories included here, "Joy and the Law" and "The Blind Kittens," reveal an author who loved nineteenth-century novels and short stories from the French and English traditions (Flaubert, Maupassant, Dickens), and liked to spend the evenings reading aloud with friends. But "The Professor and the Siren" springs from the popular lore of the island and its legacy of myth rather than its social mores or disastrous politics. The map of his native place offered Lampedusa a richly pictured mappamundi of imaginary histories: the streams, bays, mountains, promontories, lakes, and plains that carry the names of nymphs and monsters, deities and giants, and have continued to inspire writers in the long afterlife of Greek antiquity in Italy and beyond. Italo Calvino was compiling the key anthology *Italian Folktales* contemporaneously (it came out in 1956), and in his introduction he singles out, for their liveliness and invention, the stories of Agatuzza Messia, an illiterate seamstress of Messina, who had been the nurse of a Palermitan doctor, Giuseppe Pitrè. Pitrè turned himself into a pioneering ethnographer, equipping his carriage with a desk and writing materials so he could record his patients' stories; several relate encounters with beings from other worlds, including palaces under the sea. In *Beautiful Angiola*, Laura Gonzenbach, the daughter of the Swiss consul in Messina, another busy collector of local fairy tales, includes one called "La Fata Morgana" after King Arthur's sea-fairy sister who lives in the straits of Messina (north of Augusta where Lampedusa sets his tale) and rises from the depths to seduce her mortal lovers.

Lampedusa's interest in mythic territory might also owe something to his wife, Alessandra (Licy) Wolff, a Baltic aristocrat and pioneering psychoanalyst who knew half a dozen languages, including Russian and Latvian, and the traditional folklore of their cultures. "The Professor and the Siren" also adopts the symbolic, Freudian language of enchantment far more than the two other stories in this volume, which continue in Lampedusa's vein of ironic, bitter-comic, social observations.

But the fairy imagery depends even more directly on the work of Lampedusa's much-loved cousins, Lucio and Casimiro Piccolo di Calanovella. Giuseppe would stay with them for long periods in their beautiful, verdant villa by the sea at Capo d'Orlando, especially after the family palazzo in Palermo was bombed in 1943 and pretty much destroyed. All their lives, the cousins used to read aloud to one another; this custom led to the happy chance that, when Lampedusa's adopted son and heir, Gioacchino Lanza di Tomasi, was visiting in February 1957, he recorded the author reading the story on a Grundig tape recorder he had just been given by his girlfriend.

The Piccolos were gifted, celibate, quite exceptionally odd, and the only deep attachments of Giuseppe's life (apart from his mother, their aunt). Lucio was a poet and in 1954 was awarded a prize for his first collection (the story goes that he sent it to the competition in a parcel without enough stamps) by the *gran maestro* Eugenio Montale. Giuseppe accompanied Lucio to the ceremony, and the occasion, with his obscure cousin celebrated by one of the major literary figures of the day, spurred on Giuseppe to settling down properly to writing the novel *Il Gattopardo*—which he had been dreaming and planning for decades. Lucio and Giuseppe had talked books in several languages since their earliest youth, his poetical cousin championing folklore, fantasy, and poetry. Lucio corresponded with W. B. Yeats, comparing the Celtic twilight fairy folk, the Tuatha Dé Danann, with the local *fate* and sprites; he loved *The Faerie Queene* and liked to recite chunks of it at full throttle. His brother, Casimiro, was even more eccentric (as if it were possible), an artist who painted elves and phantoms, and pursued spiritualist and occult studies; his art shows how he had looked carefully at the English picture-book tradition, admiring Arthur Rackham, Edmund Dulac, and John Leech, who illustrated Hans Christian Andersen's "The Little Mermaid." "The Professor and the Siren" salutes these Piccolo cousins, I think, with Lampedusa stepping onto their terrain with unexpected vitality, in a fit of the festive communicativeness that affection for them allowed him to express.

Lampedusa is the name of a small rocky island in the southern Mediterranean, one of many in the constellation scattered across the Mediterranean around Sicily, and is the nearest Italian territory to Africa. Giuseppe Tomasi di Lampedusa never set foot on his principality. In a strange coda to his story, this islet has now become a familiar feature in the news, for it is the landing place of thousands of migrants trying to make their way—sometimes by swimming—into Europe. The mayor and citizens of the island, in a spirit of openness and adaptation, have taken it upon themselves to create a different society there in their encounter with the visitants from the sea. Lampedusa is often quoted for his cynicism about change: "If things are to remain as they are, everything has to change," says Tancredi in *The Leopard.* But it is possible, if the island of Lampedusa is today becoming an arena for fruitful social experiment in coexistence between north and south, that this famous adage can be taken in a different spirit. In the novel—as in the story about the professor—the prince encounters the unforeseen and, despite himself and all his ironical hauteur, finds riches in the transformation he undergoes.

—MARINA WARNER,
Kentish Town, 2014

FURTHER RESOURCES

Italo Calvino, editor, *Italian Folktales*, translated by George Martin (Harmondsworth: Penguin, 1982), see "The Siren Wife," 455–58.

Caterina Cardona, *Lettere a Licy* (Palermo: Sellerio, 1988).

Maria Grazia Di Paolo, "For a New Reading of Lampedusa's 'Lighea,'" *Marvels and Tales* 7, 1 (1993): 113–32.

David Gilmour, *The Last Leopard: A Life of Giuseppe Tomasi di Lampedusa* (London: Quartet, 1988).

Laura Gonzenbach, *Beautiful Angiola: The Lost Sicilian Folk and Fairy Tales*, edited and translated by Jack Zipes (London: Routledge, 2003).

Isaac Julien, *Western Union: Small Boats* (film installation, 2007).

Giuseppe Tomasi di Lampedusa, *Il Gattopardo* (Milan: Feltrinelli, 1958).

———, *I Racconti* (Milan: Feltrinelli, 1961).

———, *The Leopard*, translated by Archibald Colquhoun (London: Collins, 1961).

———, *Two Stories and a Memory*, translated by Archibald Colquhoun (London: Collins and Harvill, 1962).

———, *Voyage en Europe*, edited by Gioacchino Lanza Tomasi and Salvatore Silvano Nigro (Paris: Seuil, 2007).

Lucio Piccolo, *Canti Barocchi e altre liriche* (Milan: Mondadori, 1954).

Lucio and Casimiro Piccolo: see www.fondazionepiccolo.it.

Giuseppe Pitrè, *The Collected Sicilian Folk and Fairy Tales*, 2 volumes, edited and translated by Jack Zipes and Joseph Russo (London: Routledge, 2010).

Leonardo Sciascia, *La Scomparsa di Majorana* (Palermo: Sellerio, 1975).

———, *The Moro Affair; And: The Mystery of Majorana*, translated by Sacha Rabinovitch (New York: New York Review Books, 2004).

Gioacchino Lanza Tomasi, *Giuseppe Tomasi di Lampedusa: A Biography Through Images*, translated by Alessandro Gallenzi and J.G. Nichols (London: Alma Books, 2013).

———, introduction to a recording of Giuseppe Tomasi di Lampedusa, *La sirena* (Milan: Feltrinelli, 2014).

THE PROFESSOR AND THE SIREN

LATE IN the autumn of 1938 I came down with a severe case of misanthropy. I was living in Turin at the time, and my local girl no. 1, rifling my pockets in search of a spare fifty-lire note as I slept, had also discovered a short letter from girl no. 2. Spelling mistakes notwithstanding, it left no room for doubt concerning the nature of our relations.

My waking was both immediate and violent. Outbursts of angry dialect echoed through my modest lodgings on Via Peyron, and an attempt to scratch my eyes out was averted only by the slight twist I administered to the dear girl's left wrist. This entirely justified act of self-defense put an end to the row, but also to the romance. The girl dressed hurriedly, stuffing powder puff, lipstick, and a little handkerchief into her bag along with the fifty-lire note, "cause of so great a calamity," thrice flung a colorful local alternative to "Swine!" in my face, and left. Never had she been so adorable as in those fifteen minutes of fury. I watched from the window as she emerged and moved away into the morning mist: tall, slender, adorned with regained elegance.

I never saw her again, just as I never saw a black cashmere sweater that had cost me a small fortune and possessed the woeful merit of being cut to suit a woman just as well as a man. All she left were two of those so-called invisible hairpins on the bed.

That same afternoon I had an appointment with no. 2 in a patisserie in Piazza Carlo Felice. At the little round table in the western corner of the second room—"our" table—I saw not the chestnut tresses of the girl whom I now desired more than ever but the sly face of Tonino, her twelve-year-old brother. He'd just gulped down some hot chocolate with a double portion of whipped cream. With typical Turinese urbanity, he stood as I approached.

"Sir," he said, "Pinotta will not be coming; she asked me to give you this note. Good day, sir."

He went out, taking with him the two brioches left on his plate. The ivory-colored card announced that I was summarily dismissed on account of my infamy and "southern dishonesty." Clearly, no. 1 had tracked down and provoked no. 2, and I had fallen between two stools.

In twelve hours I had lost two usefully complementary girls plus a sweater to which I was rather attached; I also had to pick up the check for that infernal Tonino. I'd been made a fool of, humiliated in my very Sicilian self-regard; and I decided to abandon for a time the world and its pomps.

There was no better place for this period of retreat than the café on Via Po where, lonely as a dog, I now went at every free moment, and always in the evening after my work at the newspaper. It was a sort of Hades filled with the wan shades of lieutenant colonels, magistrates, and retired professors. These vain apparitions played checkers or dominoes, submerged in a light that was dimmed during the day by the clouds and the arcade outside, during the evenings by the enormous green shades on the chandeliers. They never raised their voices, afraid that any immoderate sound might upset the fragile fabric of their presence. It was, in short, a most satisfactory Limbo.

Being a creature of habit, I always sat at the same little corner table, one carefully designed to provide maximum discomfort to the customer. On my left two spectral senior officers played trictrac with two phantoms from the appeals court; their military and judicial dice slipped tonelessly from a leather cup. On my right sat an elderly man wrapped in an old overcoat with a worn astrakhan collar. He read foreign magazines one after another, smoked Tuscan cigars, and frequently spat. Every so often he would close his magazine and appear to be pursuing some memory in the spirals of smoke; then he would go back to reading and spitting. His hands were as ugly as could be, gnarled and ruddy, with fingernails that were cut straight across and not always clean. Once, however, when he came across a photograph in a magazine of an archaic Greek statue, the kind with widespread eyes and an ambiguous smile, I was surprised to see his disfigured fingertips caress the image with positively regal delicacy.

When he realized that I'd seen him, he grunted with displeasure and ordered a second espresso.

Our relations would have remained on this plane of latent hostility if not for a happy accident. Usually I left the office with five or six daily papers, including, on one occasion, the *Giornale di Sicilia*. Those were the years when the Fascist Ministry of Popular Culture, or MinCulPop, was at its most virulent, and every newspaper was just like all the others; that edition of the Palermo daily was as banal as ever, indistinguishable from a paper published in Milan or Rome, if not by its greater share of typographical errors. My reading of it was accordingly brief, and I soon set it aside on the table. I had already begun to contemplate another product of MinCulPop's vigilance when my neighbor addressed me: "Pardon me, sir, would you mind if I glanced at this *Giornale di Sicilia* of yours? I'm Sicilian, and it's been twenty years since I came across a newspaper from my part of the world." His voice was as cultivated as any I'd ever heard, the accent impeccable; his gray eyes regarded me with profound indifference.

"Be my guest. I'm Sicilian myself, you know. If you like, I can easily bring the paper every evening."

"Thank you, but that won't be necessary; my curiosity is a purely physical one. If Sicily remains as it was in my time, I imagine nothing good ever happens there. Nothing has for the past three thousand years."

He glanced through the paper, folded it, and gave it back to me, then plunged into reading a pamphlet. When he stood to go, it was clear that he hoped to slip out unnoticed, but I rose to introduce myself; he quietly muttered his name, which I failed to catch, yet neglected to extend his hand. At the threshold of the café, however, he turned, doffed his hat, and loudly shouted, "Farewell, fellow countryman." He disappeared down the arcade, leaving me speechless while the shades at their games grumbled disapprovingly.

I performed the magical rites necessary to conjure a waiter; pointing at the empty table, I asked him, "Who was that gentleman?"

"That," he replied, "is Senator Rosario La Ciura."

The name said a great deal even to an ignorant journalist. It belonged to one of the five or six Italians with an indisputable international reputation—to the most illustrious Hellenist of our time, in fact. I understood the thick magazines and the caressing of the illustration, the unsociability and hidden refinement, too.

In the newspaper offices the following day I searched through that peculiar drawer of the obituary file containing the "advancers." The "La Ciura" card was there, for once tolerably well drafted. I read how the great man had been born into an impoverished petit bourgeois family in Aci Castello (Catania), and that thanks to an astonishing aptitude for ancient Greek, and by dint of scholarships and scholarly publications, he had at the age of twenty-seven attained the chair of Greek literature at the University of Pavia. Subsequently he had moved to the University of Turin, where he remained until retirement.

He had taught at Oxford and Tübingen and traveled extensively, for not only had he been a senator since before the Fascists came to power and a member of the Lincean Academy; he had also received honorary degrees from Yale, Harvard, New Delhi, and Tokyo, as well as, of course, from the most prestigious European universities from Uppsala to Salamanca. His lengthy list of publications included many that were considered fundamental, especially those on Ionic dialects; suffice to say that he had been commissioned to edit the Hesiod volume in the Bibliotheca Teubneriana, the first foreigner so honored, to which he had added an introduction in Latin of unsurpassed scientific rigor and profundity. Finally, the greatest honor of all, he was *not* a member of the Fascist Royal Academy of Italy. What had always set him apart from other exceedingly erudite colleagues was a vital, almost carnal sense of classical antiquity, a quality on display in a collection of essays written in Italian, *Men and Gods*, which had been recognized as a work not only of great erudition but of authentic poetry. He was, in short, "an honor to a nation and a beacon to the world," as the card concluded. He was seventy-five years old and lived decorously but far from lavishly on his pension and senator's benefits. He was a bachelor.

There's no use denying that we Italians—original sons (or fathers) of the Renaissance—look on the Great Humanist as superior to all other human beings. The possibility of finding myself in daily proximity to the highest representative of such subtle, almost magical, and poorly remunerated wisdom was both flattering and disturbing. I experienced the same sensations that a young American would on meeting Mr. Gillette: fear, respect, a certain not ignoble envy.

That evening I descended into Limbo in quite a different spirit than that of the previous days. The senator was already at his spot and responded to my reverential greeting with a faint grumble. When, however, he'd finished reading an article and jotted down a few things in a small notebook, he turned toward me and, in a strangely musical voice, said, "Fellow countryman, from the manner in which you greeted me I gather that one of these phantoms has told you who I am. Forget it, and, if you haven't already done so, forget the aorist tense you studied in secondary school. Instead tell me your name, because your introduction yesterday evening was the usual mumbled mess and I, unlike you, do not have the option of learning who you are from others. Because it's clear that no one here knows you."

He spoke with insolent detachment. To him I was apparently something less than a cockroach, more like a dust mote whirling aimlessly in a sunbeam. And yet the calm voice, precise speech, and use of the familiar *tu* radiated the serenity of a Platonic dialogue.

"My name is Paolo Corbera. I was born in Palermo, where I also took my law degree. Now I work here for *La*

Stampa. To reassure you, Senator, let me add that on my exit exams I earned a '5 plus' out of 10 in Greek, and I suspect that the 'plus' was only added to make sure I received my diploma."

He gave a half smile. "Thank you for telling me this. So much the better. I detest speaking with people who think they know what they in fact do not, like my colleagues at the university. In the end they are familiar only with the external forms of Greek, its eccentricities and deformities. The living spirit of this language, foolishly called 'dead,' has not been revealed to them. *Nothing* has been revealed to them, for that matter. They are poor wretches, after all: How could they perceive this spirit without ever having had the opportunity to hear Greek?"

Pride is fine, sure, it's better than false modesty, but it seemed to me the senator was going too far. I even wondered whether the years might have succeeded in softening somewhat his exceptional mind. Those poor things, his colleagues, had had just as much opportunity to hear ancient Greek as he had—that is, none.

He went on: "Paolo, you're lucky to bear the name of the one apostle who had a bit of culture and a smattering of reading under his belt. Though Jerome would have been better. The other names you Christians carry around are truly contemptible. The names of slaves."

I was disappointed again. He really seemed like nothing more than a typical anticlerical academic with a pinch of Fascist Nietzscheism thrown in. Could it be?

His voice rose and fell appealingly as he continued to speak, with the ardor, perhaps, of someone who had passed a great deal of time in silence. "Corbera . . . Is that not one of the great names of Sicily, or am I mistaken? I remember that my father paid the annual rent for our house in Aci Castello to the administrator of a House of Corbera di Palina, or Salina, I can't recall which. He'd always joke and say that if there was one thing that was certain in this world, it was that those few lire weren't going to end up in the pockets of the 'demesne,' as he called it. But are you one of those Corberas, or just a descendant of some peasant who took his master's name?"

I confessed that I really was a Corbera di Salina, the sole surviving specimen, in fact. All the opulence, all the sins, all the uncollected rents, all the unpaid debts, all the political opportunism of the Leopard were concentrated in me alone. Paradoxically, the senator seemed pleased.

"That's fine, just fine. I have a great deal of respect for the old families. Their memory is . . . miniscule, of course, but still it's greater than the others'. It's as much of physical immortality as your sort can hope for. Think about getting married soon, Corbera, seeing as how your sort haven't found any better way to survive than scattering your seed in the strangest places."

He was definitely trying my patience. "Your sort." Who was that? The whole contemptible herd that was not fortunate enough to be Senator La Ciura? Who'd attained physical immortality? You'd never know it from looking at his wrinkled face, his sagging flesh . . .

"Corbera di Salina," he continued, undeterred, "You don't mind if I call you *tu*, as I do with my students in their fleeting youth?"

I professed to be not only honored but delighted, and I was. Moving beyond questions of names and protocol, we now spoke of Sicily. It had been twenty years since he'd set foot on the island, and the last time he'd been "down there," as he called it in the Piedmontese manner, he'd stayed a mere five days, in Syracuse, to talk to Paolo Orsi about the alternating choruses in classical theater.

"I remember they wanted to take me in a car from Catania to Syracuse; I accepted only when I learned that at Augusta the road passes far from the sea, whereas the train follows the coastline. Tell me about our island. It's a beautiful place, even if it is inhabited by donkeys. The gods once sojourned there—and perhaps in some endless Augusts they return. But don't on any account speak to me about those four modern temples of yours, not that that's anything you'd understand, I'm sure."

So we spoke about eternal Sicily, the Sicily of the natural world; about the scent of rosemary on the Nebrodi Mountains and the taste of Melilli honey; about the swaying cornfields seen from Etna on a windy day in May, some secluded spots near Syracuse, and the fragrant gusts from the citrus plantations known to sweep down on Palermo during sunset in June. We spoke of those magic summer nights, looking out over the gulf of Castellammare, when the stars are mirrored in the sleeping sea, and how, lying on your back among the mastic trees, your spirit is lost in the whirling heavens, while the body braces itself, fearing the approach of demons.

The senator had scarcely visited the island for fifty years, and yet his memory of certain minute details was remarkably precise. "Sicily's sea is the most vividly colored, the most romantic of any I have ever seen; it's the only thing you won't manage to ruin, at least away from the cities. Do the trattorias by the sea still serve spiny urchins, split in half?"

I assured him that they did, though adding that few people ate them now, for fear of typhus.

"And yet they are the most beautiful thing you have down there, bloody and cartilaginous, the very image of the female sex, fragrant with salt and seaweed. Typhus, typhus! They're dangerous as all gifts from the sea are; the sea offers death as well as immortality. In Syracuse I demanded that Orsi order them immediately. What flavor! How divine in appearance! My most beautiful memory of the last fifty years!"

I was confused and fascinated: a man of such stature indulging in almost obscene metaphors, displaying an infantile appetite for the altogether mediocre pleasure of eating sea urchins!

Our conversation stretched out, and on leaving he insisted on paying for my espresso, not without a display of his peculiar coarseness ("Everyone knows kids from good families are always broke"). We parted friends, if you disregard the fifty-year difference between our ages and the thousands of light years separating our cultures.

We proceeded to see each other every evening; even as my rage against humanity began to wane, I made it my duty never to fail to meet the senator in the underworld of Via Po. Not that we chatted much; he continued to read and take notes and only addressed me occasionally, but when he spoke it was always a melodious flow of pride and insolence, sprinkled with disparate allusions and strands of impenetrable poetry. He continued to spit as well, and eventually I observed that he did so only while he read. I believe that he also developed a certain affection for me, but I didn't delude myself. If there was affection it wasn't anything like what one of "our sort" (to adopt the senator's term) might feel for a human being; instead it was similar to what an elderly spinster might feel for her pet goldfinch, whose vacuousness and lack of understanding she is well aware of, but whose existence allows her to express aloud regrets in which the creature plays no part; and yet, if the pet were not there, she would suffer a distinct malaise. In fact, I began to notice that when I arrived late the old man's eyes, haughty as ever, were fixed on the entrance.

It took roughly a month for us to pass from topical observations—always highly original but impersonal on his part—to more indelicate subjects, which are after all the only ones that distinguish conversations between friends from those between mere acquaintances. I was the one who took the initiative. His spitting bothered me—it had also bothered the guardians of Hades, who finally brought a very shiny brass spittoon to his spot—

such that one evening I dared to inquire why he didn't seek a cure for his chronic catarrh. I asked the question without thinking and immediately regretted risking it, expecting the senatorial ire to bring the stucco work on the ceiling raining down on my head. Instead his richly toned voice replied calmly, "But my dear Corbera, I have no catarrh. You who observe so carefully should have noticed that I never cough before spitting. My spitting is not a sign of sickness but of mental health: I spit out of disgust for the rubbish I happen to be reading. If you took the trouble to examine that contrivance"—(and he gestured at the spittoon)—"you would realize that it contains hardly any saliva and no trace of mucus. My spitting is symbolic and highly cultural; if you don't like it, go back to your native drawing rooms, where people don't spit only because they can't be bothered to be nauseated by anything."

His extraordinary insolence was mitigated solely by his distant gaze; I nevertheless felt the desire to stand up and walk out on him then and there. Fortunately I had the time to reflect that the fault lay in my rashness. I stayed, and the impassive senator immediately passed to counterattack. "And you then, why patronize this Erebus full of shades and, as you say, catarrh sufferers, this locus of failed lives? In Turin there's no shortage of those creatures your sort finds so desirable. A trip to the Castello hotel in Rivoli, or to the baths in Moncalieri, and your squalid aspiration would soon be fulfilled."

I began to laugh at hearing such a cultured mouth

offer such precise information about the Turinese demimonde. "But how do you come to know about such places, Senator?"

"I know them, Corbera, I know them. Anyone spending time with politicians or members of the Academic Senate learns this, and nothing more. You will, however, do me the favor of being convinced that the sordid pleasures of your sort have never been stuff for Rosario La Ciura." One could sense that it was true: In the senator's bearing and in his words there was the unmistakable sign of a sexual reserve (as one said in 1938) that had nothing to do with age.

"The truth is, Senator, it was precisely my search for some temporary refuge from the world that first brought me here. I'd had trouble with two of just the sort of women you've so rightfully condemned."

His response was immediate and pitiless. "Betrayed, eh, Corbera? Or was it disease?"

"No, nothing like that. Worse: desertion." And I told him about the ridiculous events of two months earlier. I spoke of them in a light, facetious manner; the ulcer on my self-regard had closed, and anyone but that damned Hellenist would have teased me or possibly even sympathized. But the fearful old man did neither; instead he was indignant.

"This is what happens, Corbera, when wretched and diseased beings couple. What's more, I'd say the same to those two little trollops with respect to you, if I had the revolting misfortune to meet them."

"Diseased, Senator? Both of them were in wonderful shape; you should have seen how they ate when we dined at Gli Specchi. And as for wretched, no, not at all: Each was a magnificent figure of a young woman, and elegant as well."

The senator hissingly spat his scorn. "Diseased, I said, and made no mistake. In fifty, sixty years, perhaps much sooner, they will die; so they are already now diseased. And wretched as well. Some elegance they've got, composed of trinkets, stolen sweaters, and sweet talk picked up at the movies. Some generosity too, fishing for greasy banknotes in their lover's pockets rather than presenting him, as others do, with pink pearls and branches of coral. This is what happens when one goes in for those little monstrosities with painted faces. And were you all not disgusted—they as much as you, you as much as they—to kiss and cuddle your future carcasses between evil-smelling sheets?"

I replied stupidly, "But Senator, the sheets were always perfectly clean!"

He fumed. "What do the sheets have to do with it? The inevitable cadaver stink came from you. I repeat, how can you consent to carouse with people of their kind, of your kind?"

I, who already had my eyes on an enchanting sometime seamstress, took offense. "It's not as if one can sleep with nothing but Most Serene Highnesses!"

"Who said anything about Most Serene Highnessess? They're bound for the charnel house like the rest. But this isn't something you'd understand, young man, and I was wrong to mention it. It is fated that you and your girlfriends will wade ever further into the noxious swamps of your foul pleasures. There are very few who know better." Gazing up at the ceiling, he began to smile; a ravished expression spread over his face; then he shook my hand and left.

We didn't see each other for three days; on the fourth I received a telephone call in the editorial office. "Is this Signor Corbera? My name is Bettina Carmagnola, I'm Senator La Ciura's housekeeper. He asks me to tell you that he has had a bad cold, and that now he is better and wishes to see you tonight after dinner. Come to 18 Via Bertola at nine, second floor." The call, abruptly interrupted, became unappealable.

The building at 18 Via Bertola was a dilapidated old structure, but the senator's apartment was large and—thanks, I suppose, to the diligence of Bettina—well maintained. In the entrance hall began the parade of books, of those modest-looking, economically bound volumes found in all living libraries; there were thousands of them in the three rooms I crossed. In the fourth sat the senator, wrapped in a very ample camel-hair dressing gown that was smoother and softer than any I'd ever seen. I learned later that the fabric wasn't camel at all but was made from the precious wool of a Peruvian animal, and that the gown was a gift from the Academic Senate of Lima. The senator refrained from rising when I entered but welcomed me with considerable warmth. He was better, completely fine, in fact, and planned to be back in circulation as soon as the bitter cold spell that had descended on Turin in those days had passed. He offered me some resinous Cypriot wine, a gift from the Italian Institute of Athens; some atrocious pink *lokums* from the Archaeological Mission of Ankara; and some more sensible Turinese sweets purchased by the provident Bettina. He was in such good humor that he gave two full-mouth smiles and even went so far as to apologize for his outbursts in Hades.

"I know, Corbera, I know. I was excessive in my words, however restrained—believe me—in my concepts. Don't give it another thought."

I really didn't think about it; indeed I was full of respect for the old man, whom I suspected of being tremendously unhappy notwithstanding his triumphant career. He devoured the revolting *lokums*.

"Sweets, Corbera, ought to be sweet and nothing but. If they have another flavor they are like perverted kisses." He gave large crumbs to Aeacus, a stocky boxer that had entered the room at some point. "This creature, Corbera, for those capable of appreciating him, more closely resembles the Immortals, despite his ugliness, than your little temptresses." He refused to show me his library. "It's all classics, stuff that wouldn't interest someone like you, a moral failure in Greek." But he did lead me around the room we were in, which was his study. There were few books, among which I noted the theater of Tirso de Molina, Fouqué's *Undine*, Giraudoux's play of the same name, and, to my surprise, the works of H. G. Wells; but in compensation, on the walls, were enormous life-size photographs of archaic Greek statues, and not the typical photographs that any of us could procure for ourselves but stupendous reproductions, clearly requested with authority and sent with devotion by museums around the world. They were all there, the magnificent creatures: the Louvre's *Horseman*, the *Seated Goddess* from Taranto that is in Berlin, the *Warrior* from Delphi, one of the *Korai of the Acropolis*, the *Apollo of Piombino*, the *Lapith Woman* and the *Phoebus* from Olympia, the famous *Charioteer*... The room shone with their ecstatic and at the same time ironic smiles, gloried in the calm arrogance of their bearing. "You see, Corbera, perhaps these, if one is so fortunate; the local 'maidens,' no." Above the fireplace, ancient amphorae and craters: Odysseus tied to the mast of his boat, the Sirens casting themselves down onto the rocks in expiation for having let their prey escape. "Lies, Corbera, the lies of petit bourgeois poets. No one escapes, and even if someone did, the Sirens would never destroy themselves for so little. In any case, how could they die?"

On an end table stood a faded old photograph, simply framed, of a young man around twenty, almost nude, his curly hair disheveled, with a bold expression and features of rare beauty. Perplexed, I stopped myself for a moment. I thought I understood. Not at all. "And this, countryman, this was and is, and *will be*," he stressed, "Rosario La Ciura."

The broken-down senator in a dressing gown had been a young god.

Our conversation then turned to other matters. Before I left he showed me a letter in French from the rector of the University of Coimbra inviting him to be a guest of honor at a Greek studies conference in Portugal in May. "I'm very pleased. I'll go aboard the *Rex* in Genoa along with the French, Swiss, and German participants. Like Odysseus I'll plug my ears in order not to hear the drivel of those moral cripples, and there'll be beautiful days of sailing: the sun, the blue sky, the smell of the sea."

On my way out we again passed the shelf containing the works of Wells, and I ventured to show my surprise at seeing them there. "You're right, Corbera, they're ghastly. There's one novella there that, were I to reread it, would make me spit nonstop for a month; and even you, salon lapdog that you are, you would be appalled."

Following my visit our relations became decidedly cordial —on my part at least. I went to great lengths to have some exceptionally fresh sea urchins brought in from Genoa. When I learned that they would arrive the following day I procured some Etna wine and farmer's bread and nervously invited the senator to visit me in my tiny apartment. To my great relief he very happily accepted. I picked him up in my Fiat 508 and dragged him all the way to Via Peyron, which is something of a backwater. In the car he displayed some fear and no confidence whatsoever in my driving skills. "I know you now, Corbera; if we're unlucky enough to encounter one of your abortions in a frock, you're liable to turn your head and send us both smashing into the corner of a building." We met no skirted monstrosity worthy of note and arrived safely.

For the first time since I met him I saw the senator laugh—when we entered my bedroom. "So then, Corbera, this is the theater of your vile exploits." He examined my few books. "Fine, fine. Perhaps you're less ignorant than you seem. This one here," he added as he picked up a volume of Shakespeare, "this one here understood something. 'A sea-change into something rich and strange.'* 'What potions have I drunk of Siren tears?'"†

When the good Signora Carmagnola entered the drawing room carrying the tray of sea urchins, lemons, and the rest, the senator was ecstatic. "This was your idea? How did you know they are the thing I long for more than any other?"

"You can safely enjoy them, Senator; this morning they were still in the Ligurian Sea."

"Yes, of course, your sort are always the same, slaves to your decadence, to your putrescence; your long, asinine

*William Shakespeare, *The Tempest*, act I, scene 2.
†William Shakespeare, *The Sonnets*, 119.

ears always straining to make out the shuffling steps of Death. Poor devils! Thank you, Corbera, you've been a good famulus. It's a shame they're not from the sea down there, these urchins, that they haven't been steeped in our algae; their spines have surely never drawn a drop of divine blood. You've done what was possible, certainly, but these urchins, having dozed on the cold reefs of Nervi or Arenzano, they're almost *boreal*." It was clear that he was one of those Sicilians for whom the Ligurian Riviera—considered a tropical region by the Milanese—may as well be Iceland. The urchins, split in half, revealed their wounded, blood-red, strangely compartmentalized flesh. I'd never paid attention before now, but after the senator's bizarre comparisons they really did seem like cross sections of who knows what delicate female organs. He consumed them avidly but without cheer, with a meditative, almost sorrowful air. He didn't want to squeeze any lemon over them.

"Your sort, always combining flavors! Sea urchins have to taste also like lemon, sugar also like chocolate, love also like paradise!" When he finished he took a sip of wine and closed his eyes. After a bit I noticed, slipping from beneath his shriveled eyelids, two tears. He stood up and walked to the window, where he furtively dried his eyes. Then he turned. "Have you ever been to Augusta yourself, Corbera?" I'd spent three months there as a recruit; during off-duty hours two or three of us would take a boat out on the transparent waters and explore the gulfs. After my answer he was silent; then, in an irritated voice: "And did you grunts ever arrive as far as the inland gulf past Punta Izzo, behind the hill overlooking the saltworks?"

"We certainly did, it's the most beautiful spot in Sicily, yet to be discovered, thankfully, by the Dopolavoro crowds.* The coast is wild there, right, Senator? It's completely deserted, and you can't see a single house; the sea is the color of peacocks; and behind it all, beyond the shifting waves, rises Mount Etna. From no other spot is it so beautiful—calm, powerful, truly divine. It's a place where you can see the island in one of its eternal aspects, as it was before it so foolishly turned its back on its vocation, which was to serve as pasture for the Cattle of the Sun."

The senator was silent. Then: "You're a good kid, Corbera; if you weren't so ignorant, something might have been made of you." He came toward me and kissed my forehead. "Now bring round your jalopy. I want to go home."

In the weeks that followed we continued to see each other regularly. Now we also took late-night walks, generally down Via Po and across the martial expanse of Piazza Vittorio; we went to gaze at the rushing river and the Turin hills, elements that introduced a drop of fan-

*The Opera Nazionale Dopolavoro (National Recreational Club) was the Italian Fascist leisure and recreational organization.

tasy into the geometrical rigor of the city. Then began the spring, that affecting season of threatened youth; the first lilacs sprouted on the banks, and the most impetuous of the young couples without a place to retreat to braved the dampness of the grass. "Down there the sun already blazes, the algae blooms, the fish appear at the surface of the water on moonlit nights, and flashes of bodies can be made out between the lines of luminous foam. We stand here before this insipid, lifeless current of water, before these big ugly buildings that look like soldiers or monks all in a line, and we hear the sobs of these dying creatures coupling." It cheered him, however, to think about the impending voyage to Lisbon, not far off now. "It will be pleasant. You ought to come along as well. A shame that it's not open to those deficient in Greek; with me at least you can speak Italian, but if Zuckmayer or Van der Voos found out you didn't know the optative of every irregular verb, you'd be done for. This even though you may be more in touch with Greek reality than they are; not through cultivation, clearly, but through animal instinct."

Two days prior to his departure for Genoa he told me that he would not be returning to the café the following day, but that he would expect me at his house at nine that evening.

The protocol was identical to the last time: The images

of the gods of three thousand years ago radiated youth as a stove radiates heat; the faded photograph of the young god of fifty years ago seemed dismayed at watching his own metamorphosis into a white-haired old man sunk in an armchair.

When the Cypriot wine had been drunk the senator called Bettina and told her she could go to bed. "I will see Signor Corbera out myself when he goes." Then: "Believe me, Corbera, if I've asked you here this evening at the risk of upsetting any Rivoli fornication plans you might have had, it's because I need you. I leave tomorrow, and when you go away at my age you never know if it won't be necessary to stay away forever, especially when you go by sea. Please know that I genuinely care for you: Your ingenuousness touches me, your unconcealed carnal intrigues amuse me, and it seems to me that, as is sometimes the case with the best kind of Sicilians, you have managed to achieve a synthesis of the senses and reason. Therefore you deserve not to be left empty-handed, without hearing me explain the reason behind some of my eccentricities, of some sentences I've spoken in your presence that will certainly have appeared to you worthy of a madman."

I protested weakly: "I haven't understood many of the things you've said, but I've always attributed my incomprehension to the inadequacy of my own mind, never to an aberration of yours."

"Don't worry, Corbera, it doesn't matter. All of us old people seem crazy to you young people, and often in fact the opposite is true. To explain myself, however, I'll have to tell you about my adventure, an uncommon one. It happened when I was 'that young gentleman there,'" and he pointed at his photograph. "I have to go back to 1887, a time that will seem prehistoric to you but is not for me."

He moved from his place behind the desk and came to sit down beside me on the same couch. "Pardon me, but from now on I'll have to speak in a low voice. Important words cannot be bellowed; the 'cry of love' or hate is to be found only in melodrama or among the most uncultivated people, which comes to the same thing in the end. In 1887, then, I was twenty-four years old; I looked like the person in that photograph. I already had my degree in ancient literature and had published two articles on Ionic dialects that had caused a certain stir in my university; and for the previous year I'd been preparing for a competition for a post at the University of Pavia. Also, I had never known a woman. As a matter of fact, I have never known women either before or after that year." I was sure that my face had remained stonily impassive, but I was deceived. "Your eyelash fluttering is very ill-mannered, Corbera. What I say is the truth—the truth and a boast. I know that we Catanesi are held to be capable of impregnating our own nannies, and that may even be true. Not in my case, however. When one passes one's days and nights with goddesses and demigoddesses, as I did during that period, there remains little desire to climb the stairs of the brothels of San Berillo. At the time I was also held back by religious scruples. Corbera, you really should learn to control your eyelashes; they betray you constantly. Yes, I said religious scruples. I also said 'at the time.' Now I no longer have them; but they were worthless in any case.

"You, young Corbera, who probably obtained your position at the newspaper thanks to a note from some Party official, you don't know what it is to prepare for a competition for a university chair of Greek literature. For two years you slog away, to the limits of sanity. I already knew the language fairly well, fortunately, as well as I know it now; and I don't say so just for the sake of it, you know... But the rest: the Alexandrine and Byzantine variants of the texts; the passages cited, always poorly, from Latin authors; the countless connections between literature and mythology, history, philosophy, science! I repeat, it's enough to drive you mad. So I studied like a dog, and also gave lessons to students who'd flunked the subject, to pay the rent on my place in the city. You could say I subsisted on nothing but black olives and coffee. On top of all this came the disastrous summer of 1887, one of those truly infernal summers that we have every so often down there. At night Etna vomited back the fire of the sun that it stored up fifteen hours a day; if you touched the railing of a balcony at noon you'd have to run to the emergency room; volcanic paving stones seemed on the point of returning to their liquid state; and almost every day the sirocco swatted you in the face with sticky bats' wings. I was on the verge of collapse when a friend came to my aid. He found me wandering the streets, exhausted, muttering Greek verses I no longer understood. My appearance troubled him. 'Look, Rosario, if you stay here you'll go mad, and then so much for the competition. Myself, I'm off to Switzerland'—the fellow had money—'but in Augusta I've got a three-room cabin twenty yards from the sea, far from the village. Pack a bag, take your books, and go stay there for the rest of the summer. Come by my place in an hour and I'll give you the key. Just wait till you see, it's something else. Ask for the Carobene place at the station, everyone knows it. But you've really got to leave—tonight.'

"I followed his advice and left that same evening. On awaking the next morning, rather than the toilet pipes across the courtyard that used to greet me at dawn, I found before me a pure expanse of sea, and beyond it a no longer pitiless Etna, wrapped in the morning mist. The spot was completely deserted, as you said it still is now, and of a singular beauty. The little house's dilapidated rooms contained just the sofa on which I'd slept, a table, and three chairs; the kitchen, a few earthenware pots and an old lamp. Behind the house were a fig tree and a well. Paradise. I went into the village and tracked down the farmer of the small Carobene estate, and worked out that every few days he would bring me some bread, pasta, vegetables, and kerosene. Olive oil I had, from the supply my poor mother had sent me in Catania. I rented a dinghy that the fisherman brought round that afternoon along with a wicker fish basket and a few hooks. I'd decided to stay there for at least two months.

"Carobene was right: It really was something else.

The heat was violent in Augusta too, but, no longer reflected back by walls, it produced not dreadful prostration but a sort of submissive euphoria; the sun, shedding its executioner's grimace, was content to be a smiling if brutal giver of energy, and also a sorcerer setting mobile diamonds in the sea's slightest ripple. Study ceased to be toil: Gently rocked by the boat in which I spent hours on end, each book seemed no longer an obstacle to be overcome but rather a key offering me passage into a world, a world I already had before my eyes in one of its most enchanting aspects. I often happened to recite the verses of poets aloud, and thus the names of those gods, which most people have forgotten or never knew, again skimmed the surface of the sea that would have once, at their mere mention, risen up in turmoil or subsided into dead calm.

"My isolation was absolute, interrupted only by visits from the farmer who brought me my few provisions every three or four days. He would only stay for five minutes; seeing me so exhilarated and disheveled, he must have thought me dangerously close to madness. And in truth, the sun, the seclusion, the nights passed beneath the wheeling stars, the silence, the scant nourishment, the study of remote subjects wove around me a spell that predisposed me to marvels.

"This came to pass on the morning of August 5, at six o'clock. I hadn't been up for long before I was in the boat; a few strokes of the oars took me away from the pebbled shore. I'd stopped at the base of a large rock whose shadow might protect me from a sun that was already climbing, swollen with dazzling fury and turning the whiteness of the auroral sea gold and blue. As I declaimed I sensed that the side of the boat, to my right and behind me, had abruptly been lowered, as if someone had grabbed on to climb up. I turned and saw her: The smooth face of a sixteen-year-old emerged from the sea; two small hands gripped the gunwale. The adolescent smiled, a slight displacement of her pale lips that revealed small, sharp white teeth, like dogs'. This, however, was not a smile like those to be seen among your sort, always debased with an accessory expression of benevolence or irony, of compassion, cruelty, or whatever the case may be; it expressed nothing but itself: an almost bestial delight in existing, a joy almost divine. This smile was the first of her charms that would affect me, revealing paradises of forgotten serenity. From her disordered hair, which was the color of the sun, seawater dripped into her exceedingly open green eyes, over features of infantile purity.

"Our suspicious reason, howsoever predisposed, loses its bearings in the face of the marvelous, and when it perceives it, tries to rely on the memory of banal phenomena. Like anyone else would have, I supposed that I'd met a swimmer. Moving cautiously, I pulled myself up to her level, leaned toward her, and held out my hands to help her aboard. Instead she rose with astonishing strength straight out of the water to her waist, encircled my neck with her arms, wrapping me in a never before experienced perfume, and allowed herself to be pulled into the boat. Her body below the groin, below the buttocks, was that of a fish, covered with tiny pearly blue scales and ending in a forked tail that slapped gently against the bottom of the boat. She was a Siren.

"She lay back, resting her head on interlaced fingers, displaying with serene immodesty the delicate little hairs of her armpits, her splayed breasts, her perfect stomach. She exuded what I have clumsily referred to as a perfume, a magical smell of the sea, of decidedly youthful sensuality. We were in the shade but twenty yards from us the seashore reveled in the sun and quivered with pleasure. My near-complete nudity ill concealed my own emotion.

"She spoke and thus was I overwhelmed, after her smile and smell, by the third and greatest of her charms: her voice. It was a bit guttural, husky, resounding with countless harmonics; behind the words could be discerned the sluggish undertow of summer seas, the whisper of receding beach foam, the wind passing over lunar tides. The song of the Sirens, Corbera, does not exist; the music that cannot be escaped is their voice alone.

"She spoke Greek and I struggled to understand her. 'I heard you speaking to yourself in a language similar to my own. I like you: take me. I am Lighea, daughter of Calliope. Don't believe the stories about us. We don't kill anyone, we only love.'

"I bent over her as I rowed, staring into her smiling eyes. When we reached the shore I took her aromatic body into my arms and we passed from the blazing sun into the deep shade; there she poured into my mouth such sensual pleasure that it is to your terrestrial kisses as wine is to insipid water."

The senator narrated his adventure in a low voice. I who in my heart had always set my own varied experiences with women against those he regarded as mediocre, and had derived from this a foolish sense of reduced distance, was humiliated: in matters of love as well, I saw myself sunk to unfathomable depths. Never for a moment did I suspect he was lying to me, and had anyone else been there, even the most skeptical of witnesses, he too would have perceived the certainty of truth in the old man's tone.

"So began those three weeks. I have no right, nor would it be merciful to you, to go into details. Suffice to say that in those embraces I enjoyed the highest form of spiritual pleasure along with the greatest physical gratification, devoid of any social resonance, the same that our solitary mountain shepherds experience when they couple with their goats. If the comparison repels you, it's because you're not capable of performing the necessary transposition from the bestial to the superhuman plane—planes that were, in this case, superimposed.

"Think about how much Balzac dared not express in 'Une Passion dans le désert.' From her immortal limbs flowed such life force that any loss of energy was immediately compensated, increased, in fact. In those days, Corbera, I loved as much as a hundred of your Don Juans put together, over their entire lives. And what love!

Sheltered from conventions and crimes, the rancor of commendatori and the triviality of Leporellos, far from the claims of the heart, the lying sighs, the phony melting weakness that inevitably mark your sort's wretched kisses. To be honest, a Leporello did disturb us the first day, and it was the only time: Around ten I heard the sound of the farmer's boots on the path that leads down to the sea; just in time, with the farmer at the door, I managed to throw a sheet over the uncommon body of Lighea. Her uncovered head, throat, and arms led our Leporello to believe this was some commonplace affair and hence commanded his sudden respect. His stay was shorter than usual. As he went he winked his left eye, and with his right thumb and index finger at the corner of his mouth made the motion of curling an imaginary mustache; and he returned up the path.

"I spoke of our having spent twenty days together. However, I wouldn't want you to imagine that during those three weeks she and I lived, as they say, 'conjugally,' sharing our bed, meals, and occupations. Lighea's absences were quite frequent. Without any advance notice she would dive into the sea and disappear, sometimes for many hours. When she returned, almost always first thing in the morning, either she found me in the boat or, if I was still in the cabin, wriggled up the pebbled shore till she was half out of the water, on her back and pushing with her arms, calling to be helped up the slope. 'Sasà,' she would call, because I'd told her this was the diminutive form of my name. In this maneuver, made awkward by the same part of her body that granted her agility in the sea, she gave the pitiable impression of a wounded animal, an impression immediately obliterated by the smile in her eyes.

"She ate nothing that was not alive. I often saw her rise out of the sea, delicate torso sparkling in the sun, teeth tearing into a still-quivering silver fish, blood running down her chin; after a few bites the mangled hake or bream would be tossed over her shoulder and sink into the water, staining it red, while she shouted in childish delight and ran her tongue over her teeth. Once I gave her some wine. Drinking from a glass was impossible for her, so I was obliged to pour some into her small and slightly greenish hand; she lapped up the liquid as dogs do, her eyes registering surprise at the unfamiliar flavor. She said it was good but afterward always refused it. From time to time she came to shore with hands full of oysters or mussels, and while I struggled to open the shells with a knife, she crushed them with a stone and sucked down the throbbing mollusk along with bits of shell that did not trouble her in the least.

"I told you before, Corbera: She was a beast and at the same time an Immortal, and it's a shame that we cannot continuously express this synthesis in speaking, the way she does, with absolute simplicity, in her own body. Not only did she display in the carnal act a cheerfulness and a delicacy altogether contrary to wretched animal lust, but her speech was of a powerful immediacy, the likes of which I have only ever found in a few great poets. Not for nothing was she the daughter of Calliope: Oblivious to all cultures, ignorant of all wisdom, disdainful of any moral constraint whatsoever, she was nevertheless part of the source of all culture, of all knowledge, of all ethics, and she knew how to express this primitive superiority of hers in terms of rugged beauty. 'I am everything because I am only the stream of life, free of accident. I am immortal because all deaths converge in me, from that of the hake just now to that of Zeus; gathered in me they once again become life, not individual and particular but belonging to nature and thus free.' Then she said, 'You are young and handsome. You should follow me into the sea now and escape sorrows and old age. You would come to my home beneath enormous mountains of motionless dark water, where all is silent calm so innate that those who possess it no longer even perceive it. I have loved you, and so remember: When you are tired, when you can truly bear it no longer, all you have to do is lean out over the sea and call me. I will always be there, because I am everywhere, and your dream of sleep will be fulfilled.'

"She told me about her life below the sea, about bearded Tritons and glaucous caverns, but she said that these too were vain appearances and that the truth lay much deeper indeed, in the blind, mute palace of formless, eternal waters, without sparkle, without murmurs.

"Once she told me she would be away for some time, until the evening of the following day. 'I must travel far, to where I know I will find a gift for you.'

"In fact she returned with a stupendous branch of

deep red coral encrusted with shells and algae. For a long while I kept it in a drawer and every night I would kiss the spots where I recalled the Indifferent, that is the Beneficent, one had placed her fingers. Then one day my housekeeper, Maria—Bettina's predecessor—stole it to give to one of her pimps. I later found it in a Ponte Vecchio jeweler's shop, deconsecrated, cleaned up and smoothed to the point of being virtually unrecognizable. I bought it back and that same night threw it into the Arno: It had passed through too many profane hands.

"She also spoke to me of the many human lovers she'd had during her thousand-year adolescence: fishermen and sailors—Greeks, Sicilians, Arabs, Capresi—including survivors of shipwrecks clinging to sodden debris, to whom she'd appeared in a flash of lightning during a storm to transform their last gasp into pleasure. 'They all accepted my invitation and came to see me, some immediately, others after having lived what to them seemed a long time. Only one failed to show. He was a big beautiful young man with red hair and exceptionally white skin; I joined myself to him on a beach far away, where our sea flows into the great Ocean. He smelled of something stronger than the wine you gave me the other day. I believe that he failed to show not, surely, because he was happy, but because when we met he was so drunk as not to understand anything anymore. I must have seemed like one of his usual fisherwomen.'

"Those weeks of high summer flew by as rapidly as a single morning; when they'd passed I realized that in fact I had lived centuries. That lascivious girl, that cruel little beast, had also been the wisest of Mothers; with her mere presence she'd uprooted faiths, dispelled metaphysics; with her fragile, often bloodstained fingers she'd shown me the path toward true eternal peace, and also toward an asceticism based not on sacrifice but on the impossibility of accepting other, inferior pleasures. I will certainly not be the second man to fail to heed her call, will not refuse this sort of pagan Grace that has been granted me.

"In accordance with its own violence, that summer was short. Not long after August 20 the first clouds timidly gathered; a few isolated blood-warm drops of rain fell. The nights brought to the distant horizon slow mute flashes of lightning, deduced one from the other like the cogitations of a god. Mornings the dove-gray sea suffered for its hidden restlessness; evenings it rippled without any perceptible breeze, in gradations from smoke gray to steel gray to pearl gray, all extremely soft colors and more affectionate than the splendor before. Faraway shreds of fog skimmed the water; on the coasts of Greece, perhaps, it was already raining. The color of Lighea's mood also changed, from radiance to gray affection. She was silent more often; spent hours stretched out on a rock, staring at the no longer motionless horizon; spent less time away. 'I want to stay here longer with you; if I were to take to the open sea now my marine companions would keep me there. Do you hear them? They're calling me.' At times I truly did seem to hear a different, lower note among the seagull calls, to make out flashes of movement from rock to rock. 'They're blowing their conches, calling Lighea to the festival of the storm.'

"This set upon us at dawn on the twenty-sixth day. From our rock we saw the approaching wind as it battered distant waters; closer by, sluggish leaden waves swelled ever larger. Soon the gusts arrived, whistling in our ears, bending the withered rosemary bushes. The sea churned below us and the first white-capped surge advanced. 'Farewell, Sasà. You won't forget.' The billow broke upon the rock; the Siren dove into the iridescent spray. I never saw her come down; she seemed to dissolve into the foam."

The senator left the next morning; I went to the station to see him off. He was surly and cutting as usual, but, when the train began to move, his fingers reached through the window to graze my head.

The next day at dawn a telephone call came into the newspaper from Genoa: During the night Senator La Ciura had fallen into the sea from the deck of the *Rex* as it sailed toward Napoli; though lifeboats had been deployed immediately, the body was not found.

A week later came the reading of his will: To Bettina went the bank account and furniture; the library was donated to the University of Catania; in a recently added codicil I was named legatee of both the Greek crater with the Siren figures and the large photograph of the Acropolis kore.

I had the two objects sent to my house in Palermo. Then came the war and while I was stuck in Marmarica with a pint of water a day, the "Liberators" destroyed my house. When I returned I found the photograph had been cut into strips and used by the looters for torches. The crater had been smashed to bits; the largest piece showed the feet of Odysseus tied to the mast of his ship. I still have it today. The books had been stored underground by the university, but, for lack of money for shelves, there they slowly rot.

JOY AND THE LAW

WHEN HE climbed aboard the bus, he annoyed everyone.

The briefcase bulging with other people's papers, the enormous package crammed beneath his left arm, his plush gray scarf, the umbrella threatening to open—all this made it difficult for him to show his return ticket. Obliged to rest the package on the driver's change table, he sent scores of coins cascading to the floor; when he tried to kneel down to retrieve them, protests rose behind him from those afraid his delay would cause their coattails to catch in the automatically closing door. He managed to insert himself into the line of people clinging to the bars overhead; slight of build though he was, his bundles conferred upon him the volume of a nun swelled up with seven skirts. As they skidded on the slush through the miserable chaos of the traffic, his awkward bulk spread discontent from one end of the vehicle to the other: He stepped on toes, had his own stepped on, and prompted reproaches; when he even heard slyly muttered allusions to his alleged conjugal misfortunes, honor compelled him to turn his head; he flattered himself that he lodged a threat in the weary expression of his eyes.

Meanwhile they traveled through streets whose rustic

baroque façades obscured a wretched hinterland that nonetheless contrived to peek out at every corner. They passed the faintly yellow lights of octogenarian shops.

Approaching his stop, he rang the bell, tripped over his umbrella as he got off, finally found himself alone on his own square yard of uneven sidewalk; he hastened to verify the presence of his plastic wallet. And was free to savor his happiness.

Contained in the wallet was 37,245 lire, the year-end bonus he'd received an hour earlier, amounting to the removal of several thorns from his family's side: his landlord, to whom he owed two quarters' rent, growing more insistent the longer he was thwarted; the exceedingly punctual collector of installment payments on his wife's *veste de lapin* ("It suits you much better than a long coat, my dear, it's slimming"); the black looks of the fishmonger and greengrocer. The five large banknotes likewise eliminated his dread of the next light bill, the dismayed stares at the children's shoes, the anxious watch for flickers in the bottled-gas flame; the notes hardly represented opulence, to be sure, but they did promise a respite from anguish, which is the true joy of the poor; and perhaps a few thousand lire would survive long enough to be consumed in the splendor of Christmas dinner.

But too many such bonuses had come and gone for him to mistake the fleeting exhilaration produced by them for the euphoria now welling up inside him, rosy and bright. Rosy, yes, rosy like the wrapping of the delicious weight that was making his left arm sore. Indeed, it was precisely from the fifteen-pound panettone he had carried away from the office that the feeling emanated. Not that he was crazy about that reliably mediocre mixture of flour, sugar, egg powder, and raisins. On the contrary, to be honest he didn't even like it. But fifteen pounds of a luxury good all at once! An immense if circumscribed instance of abundance in a house where food typically entered in quarter pounds and pints! An illustrious product in a pantry dedicated to third-rate generics! What joy for Maria! What a thrill for the children, who for two whole weeks would venture into that unknown land of the afternoon snack!

These, however, were the joys of others, material joys composed of vanillin and colored cardboard, of panettones, in other words. His personal happiness was something else entirely, a spiritual happiness mixed with pride and tenderness—yessir, spiritual.

Earlier that day when the commendatore in charge of his office had distributed pay envelopes and Christmas wishes with the haughty bonhomie of the old Fascist party official that he was, he'd also said that the fifteen-pound panettone presented to the office by Central Manufacturing would be conferred on the most deserving employee, and thus he entreated his dear staff to democratically (his word) select the lucky man straightaway.

The panettone, meanwhile, stood at the center of his desk, hermetically sealed, "laden with good omens," as the commendatore himself would have said twenty years ago in his black uniform of Sardinian wool. Giggles and whispers had passed from colleague to colleague; then everyone, starting with the director, had shouted his name. A source of great satisfaction, an assurance of continued employment—in short, a triumph. And nothing could have dampened that invigorating sensation, not the three hundred lire he'd had to spend at the wretched "café" below, in the double bruising of a blustery sunset and low-pressure neon, when he'd treated his friends to coffee, nor the swearing he'd had directed at him on the bus—nothing, not even the abrupt realization deep in his consciousness that it had come down to a moment of scornful pity for the neediest among the employees. He truly was too poor to permit the weed of pride to sprout where it could not survive.

He set off home along a decrepit street to which the bombardments of fifteen years earlier had provided the finishing touches. He arrived in the ghostly little piazza at whose far edge squatted the phantasmal building.

He vigorously greeted the concierge, Cosimo, who despised him for earning less than he did. Nine steps, three steps, nine steps: the floor where the gentleman So-and-So lived. Phooey! He had a Fiat 1100, it's true, but he also had an ugly and licentious old wife. Nine steps, three steps, a slip and near stumble, nine steps: the apartment of Dr. What's-His-Name. Worse than ever! A layabout son who went crazy for Lambretta and Vespa scooters and a waiting room that was always empty. Nine steps, three steps, nine steps: his own apartment, the modest residence of a well-liked and honest man, an esteemed prizewinner, an outstanding accountant.

He opened the door and penetrated the tiny entrance hall already filled with the smell of frying onions and herbs. On a wooden chest as large as a hamper he set down the weighty package, the briefcase loaded with other people's business, the unwieldy scarf. His voice blared out, "Maria! Come quick! Come and see what bounty I have brought!"

His wife emerged from the kitchen in a sky-blue housecoat stained with soot from the pots, her small, dishwater-reddened hands resting on a stomach deformed by multiple births. The children, snot trailing from noses, huddled around the rose-colored monument and squealed without daring to touch it.

"Nicely done! And your salary as well? I haven't got a lira left myself."

"Here it is, dear. I'm keeping just the coins for myself, two hundred forty-five lire. Now, by God, take a look at this!"

Maria had once been pretty, and until a few years ago she'd had a sweet, expressive face illuminated by capricious eyes. Since then, squabbles with shopkeepers had hoarsened her voice, poor food had ruined her complexion, the incessant scanning of a horizon filled with fog and reefs had extinguished the brilliance of her eyes. All that survived in her was a saintly soul, inflexible and without tenderness; a profound goodness reduced to expressing itself in reproaches and prohibitions; and a pride of caste, mortified but tenacious, because she was the granddaughter of a celebrated hatter on Via Indipendenza and despised the less distinguished origins of her Girolamo, whom she nonetheless adored as one does a dull but endearing child.

Her gaze slid dispassionately over the delightful package.

"Very good. Tomorrow we'll send it to Risma. We owe him a favor."

Two years ago the lawyer Risma had hired him for a complicated accounting job, and, in addition to paying him, had invited them both to lunch in his abstractionist, metallic apartment, where the accountant had suffered like a dog in the new shoes he'd bought especially for the occasion. And now, for the sake of this litigator who lacked for nothing, his dear Maria, his boys Andrea and Saverio, his baby daughter Giuseppina, he himself, all forced to surrender the only vein of abundance discovered in so many years!

He ran into the kitchen, grabbed a knife, and rushed to sever the golden twine some industrious Milanese worker had so handsomely knotted atop the wrapping, but a reddened hand fell wearily on his shoulder.

"Don't be a child, Girolamo. You know that we have to return Risma's favor."

It was the Law that spoke, the Law decreed by irreproachable hatters.

"But darling, this is a prize, a token of appreciation, a badge of merit!"

"Let it go. Your colleagues are hardly ones for noble sentiments! It's charity, Girì, nothing but charity." She called him by his old pet name, smiled at him with eyes in which he alone could perceive the traces of her former charms.

"Tomorrow we'll buy another panettone, a little one, which is plenty for us, and four of those red corkscrew candles they've got in the window at Standa; that'll make it a special holiday."

And so the next day he bought a tiny, nondescript panettone, not four but two of the astonishing candles, and engaged an agency to send the colossus to the lawyer Risma, costing him a further two hundred lire.

After Christmas, moreover, he was obliged to purchase a third cake, which, disguised in slices, he had to bring in for the colleagues who'd teased him about not offering them a single crumb of the sumptuous booty.

The fate of the original panettone was thereafter obscured by a curtain of fog.

He went to the agency, Lightning Couriers, to complain. He was grudgingly shown the delivery receipt whose reverse side the lawyer's servant had signed. After Epiphany, however, a visiting card arrived: "With warmest thanks and holiday wishes."

Honor had been preserved.

THE BLIND KITTENS

THE MAP of the Ibba family properties, drawn at 1:5000 scale, occupied a strip of waxed paper six and a half feet long and thirty-two inches high. Not that everything on it belonged to the family. First of all, to the south there was a sliver of sea running along a coast strewn with tuna fisheries that did not belong to anyone; to the north there were inhospitable mountains the Ibbas had never wanted to lay hands on; there were, above all, numerous and not insignificant white areas surrounding the lemon-yellow mass that represented the family's property holdings: lands never acquired because their owners were rich, lands offered for sale but refused on account of their poor quality, lands desired but still in the hands of people being worked on who had yet to become suitably flexible. There were also a very few lands that had once been yellow but had reverted to white because they'd been sold to buy other, better lands during certain bad harvest years when farmers were scarce. Notwithstanding these areas (all at the margins), the yellow body was impressive: From an ovoid nucleus around Gibilmonte a wide branch extended east, narrowed, then broadened again and sent forth two tentacles, one toward the sea, which it reached after a short stretch, the other northward and ending at the foot of the craggy, barren mountains. Westward expansion had been even greater. These were former Church lands, into which the advance had been as fast as a headlong fall, like a knife in lard: The villages of San Giacinto and San Narciso had been breached and overrun by acts of expropriation, the defensive line of the Favarotta River had been held for some time but finally collapsed, and today, September 14, 1901, a bridgehead had been established beyond the river through the purchase of Píspisa, a small but succulent estate bordering the pebbled right bank.

The newly acquired property had yet to be colored yellow on the map, but the India ink and tiny brush waited in the writing desk for the intervention of Calcedonio, the only one in the house who knew how to use them properly. Don Batassano Ibba himself, the head of the family and virtually a baron, had tried ten years ago following the capture of Scíddico, with lamentable results: A sea of pale yellow had washed over the entire map, and he'd had to spend a heap of money to have another one made. The bottle of ink, though, was still the same. On this occasion, therefore, Don Batassano did not risk meddling with it and settled for gazing, with his impudent farmer's eyes, at the space to be colored in, and thought that now, even on a map of all of Sicily, it would be possible to make out the Ibba lands, no bigger than a flea in the island's vastness, of course, and yet clearly visible.

Don Batassano was satisfied but also irritated, two moods that often coexisted in him. The Prince of Salina's lawyer, Ferrara, having arrived that morning from Palermo to draw up the bill of sale, had been captious up until the moment of signing—what am I saying, up until the signing! after as well!—and he'd wanted the sum in eighty big pink Bank of Sicily notes instead of the letter of credit that had already been prepared; and he, Don Batassano, had been forced to climb the stairs and remove the bundle from the most secret drawer of his personal desk, an extremely anxious operation, because at that hour it was possible that Mariannina and Totò were about. It's true that the lawyer had allowed himself to be fooled with respect to the annual fee of eighty lire payable to the Church fund, for which he had agreed to issue 1,600 lire of capitalized value, while Don Batassano (and the notary) knew it had already been paid off nine years earlier by another Salina lawyer. But this wasn't important; even minimal opposition to his will, especially concerning money, exasperated him: "They're up to their necks in debt, forced to sell, and still they take it into their heads to discriminate between banknotes and letters of credit!"

It was only four o'clock and dinner wasn't until five. Don Batassano opened the window that overlooked the meager courtyard. Into the dim room slipped the sultriness of a September seared, baked, and steeped. Down below, an old mustachioed man spread birdlime on lengths of cane, creating amusements for the don's children.

"Giacomino, saddle the horses, mine as well as yours. I'm coming down."

He wished to go see the damage done to the drinking trough in Scíddico; some young vandals had broken one of the basin's coping stones, they'd told him that morning. The crack had already been hastily filled with crushed stone and that mixture of mud and straw that can always be found near where animals drink, but Tano, the leaseholder for Scíddico, had asked for a proper repair to be made immediately. Always new nuisances, new excuses, and if he didn't go in person, the laborer would present him with an extortionate bill. He checked that his holster with the heavy Smith & Wesson hung from his belt: He was so accustomed to having the pistol with him that he no longer noticed its presence. He went down the slate stairs to the courtyard. The field warden was finishing saddling the horses. He climbed onto his horse, making use of three stone steps placed against a wall for that purpose, took the crop a boy held out to him, and waited for Giacomino to mount (without the aid of the master's stairs). The warden's son threw open the fortified gate, the summer afternoon light flooded the courtyard, and Don Batassano Ibba and his bodyguard rode out onto the main street of Gibilmonte.

The two men proceeded nearly side by side, Giacomino's horse only half a head behind his master's. The warden's "two shot" presented, to the right and left of the saddlebow, its ironclad stock and burnished barrels; the beasts' hooves shuffled arrhythmically on the cobbles of the steep lanes. Women spun thread in front of their doors and did not greet them.

"Mind the horses!" shouted Giacomino from time to time, when some tiny, entirely naked child looked set to tumble between the animals' legs. The archpriest, perched in his chair, head resting against the wall of the church, feigned sleep—in any case, the institution did not belong to the fat cat Ibba but to the poor and absent Santapau. Only the carabinieri sergeant, standing in shirtsleeves on the barracks balcony, inclined his head in greeting. They left the town and climbed the cattle track that led to the watering place. A great deal of water had been lost during the night, and a large puddle had formed around the trough. Mixed with clay, with bits of straw, with cow dung and urine, it gave off a powerful ammoniac smell. But the improvised repair had been effective: water no longer flowed through the joints between the stones but merely beaded there, and the thin stream that fitfully poured from the rusty pipe outpaced the loss. The zero cost of what had been done was gratifying to Don Batassano, causing him to overlook the provisional nature of the repair.

"What was Tano going on about, the trough is in fine shape! It doesn't need a thing more. In fact, you tell that idiot, if he's truly a man, not to let my property be damaged by the first snotty brat to happen by. Try to find their fathers and get them to speak to you, if he can't manage it himself."

On the way back a frightened rabbit crossed their

path, spooking Don Batassano's horse and causing it to kick out, and the magnate, who sat astride a handsome English saddle but used loops of rope in place of stirrups, ended up on the ground. He wasn't hurt, and Giacomino, an expert in such things, took the mare by the reins and held her still. Don Batassano, still on the ground, bitterly whipped the snout, ears, and flanks of the animal, which trembled continually and foamed at the mouth. A kick in the stomach concluded the pedagogic exercise. Don Batassano remounted and the two men returned home just as it began to grow dark.

The lawyer Ferrara, meanwhile, unaware that the master of the house had gone out, entered the study and, finding it empty, sat down a moment to wait. In the room was a rack with two rifles, a shelf with a small number of files ("Taxes," "Title Deeds," "Sureties," "Loans" read the labels stuck to the brown cardboard); on the desk the bill of sale signed two hours earlier; on the wall behind, the map.

Ferrara stood up to take a closer look. From his professional experience, from countless indiscretions overheard, he knew well how that enormous mass of property had been assembled: an epic tale of cunning, of lack of scruples, of defiance of the laws, of implacability and also luck, of daring as well. Ferrara considered what interest might have been offered by a differently tinged map, one where, as in the textbooks that showed the Italian expansion of the House of Savoy, successive acquisitions were indicated by different colors. Here, in Gibilmonte, was the embryo: six *tumuli*, about one and a half acres, plus an acre of vineyards and a three-room cottage, everything that Don Batassano's illiterate genius father, Gaspare, had inherited. When still very young Gaspare had seduced the deaf-mute daughter of a local "bourgeois," a minor landowner only slightly poorer than he was, and with the dowry obtained by means of the extorted marriage had doubled his own assets. The disabled wife, Marta, had entered fully into her husband's game: A sordid meanness permitted the couple to put together a small sum that was nonetheless significant in a place like Sicily, where the economy in that period was, as in the ancient city-states, founded exclusively on usury.

The couple made extremely shrewd loans, in particular to persons in possession of property but without sufficient income to cover interest payments. Marta's moans, as she made the rounds of the village to demand her weekly payments, had become proverbial: "When Marta goes a-grumbling, the houses go a-tumbling." In ten years of gesticulating visits, ten years of stealing wheat from the Santapau marquis (to whom Gaspare was tenant farmer), ten years of cautiously shifted boundaries, ten years of gratified appetite, the couple's property holdings had grown fivefold. He was only twenty-eight years old; the current Don Batassano, seven. There had been a rough period after the Bourbon judicial authority had taken it upon itself to investigate one of the bodies that turned up regularly in the fields; Gaspare had had to keep away from Gibilmonte, and his wife spread the word that he was staying with a cousin in Adernò in order to learn how to cultivate mulberries; in fact not a night passed in which the affectionate Gaspare did not watch from the nearby mountains as the smoke rose from the kitchen of his cheerful little house. Then came the *Mille*, Garibaldi's thousand-man volunteer army: Everything was turned upside down, the troublesome documents disappeared from the public records office, and Gaspare Ibba officially returned home.

Everything was better than ever. It was then that Gaspare conceived a mad maneuver, mad as every act of genius is: Just as Napoleon at Austerlitz dared to hollow out his own center in order to ensnare the foolish Austro-Russians with his powerful flanks, so Gaspare mortgaged all his hard-won patches of earth to the hilt, and with the few lire obtained through this operation made a zero-interest loan to the Marquis Santapau, who was in a tight spot owing to his financial contributions to the Bourbon cause. This was the result: After two years the Santapaus had lost the Balate estate, which they had in any case never seen and which, based on the name—which meant "paving stones" in the local dialect—they presumed infertile; the mortgages on the Ibba properties were lifted, Gaspare became Don Gaspare, and his family dined on mutton every Saturday and Sunday. Once he arrived at his first 100,000 lire, everything proceeded like clockwork: He acquired Church properties for a tenth of their value by paying the first two installments of their pitiful appraisals; owning these groups of houses, the springs that ran through them, the rights of way that they controlled, made the purchase of depreciated lay properties nearby wonderfully easy; the considerable income derived from these allowed for the purchase or expropriation of other, more distant estates.

When Don Gaspare died young, his holdings were nevertheless more than respectable; like the Prussian territories of the mid-eighteenth century, they consisted of large islands separated by others' properties. To his son, as to Frederick II, fell the burden and the glory of unifying it all in a single block, and then of expanding the limits of this block toward ever more distant horizons. Vineyards, olive and almond groves, pastures and emphyteutic rents, and, above all, arable land were annexed and assimilated; their revenues flowed into the humble study in Gibilmonte, where they remained only briefly, soon departing, nearly intact, to be transformed again into land. A wind of uninterrupted fortune swelled the sails of the galleon Ibba, and the name began to be uttered with reverence in every corner of the impoverished island's triangle. Don Batassano meanwhile had been married, at the age of thirty, and not to a handicapped woman like his esteemed mother but to a robust eighteen-year-old, Laura, the daughter of Gibilmonte's notary, who brought a dowry of her own good health, a considerable amount of money, valuable lessons in sophistry from her father, and a submission to his authority that, once her own not insignificant sexual needs were satisfied, was absolute. Eight children were the living proof of this submission; a bitter happiness, deprived of light, reigned in Casa Ibba.

The lawyer Ferrara was a tenderhearted man, an extremely rare type of human being in Sicily. His father had been a member of the Salina administration during the turbulent times of the old Prince Fabrizio, and he himself, raised in the muffled atmosphere of that household, had grown accustomed to desiring a life that was perhaps mediocre, but calm. He was content to gnaw at his own little piece of princely cheese. Those not quite two square yards of waxed paper evoked for him asperities and stubborn struggles that revolted his rodent's—rather more than carnivore's—soul. He had the impression of rereading the installments of *The History of the Bourbons of Naples* that his father, a fervent liberal, would buy him every week. At Gibilmonte, moreover, there wasn't anything like the alleged orgies of Caserta described in the booklets; here everything was rugged, practical, puritanically wicked. He took fright and left the room.

That evening at dinner the entire family was in attendance, except the eldest son, Gaspare, who was in Palermo for the ostensible purpose of preparing to repeat his secondary-school exit exams (he was already twenty). The meal was served with rustic simplicity, with all the cutlery—heavy and ornate though it was—placed in a pile at the center of the table, leaving everyone to fish out what they needed; the servants Totò and Mariannina insisted on serving from the right. The lady Laura was the picture of health in its fullest flower, that is to say, its supreme corpulence: Her voluptuous chin, Gentile nose, and eyes experienced in conjugal passion disappeared into a bloom of lard alluringly fresh and firm; her enormous forms were clothed in black silk, the mark of continually renewed sorrows. Her sons Melchiorre, Pietro, and Ignazio each sat between two of her daughters, Marta, Franceschina, Assunta, and Paolina, every sibling's manifest family resemblance a peculiar mixture of the father's rapacious features and the mother's merciful ones. None paid any attention to dress: gray-on-white printed cretonnes for the girls, sailor suits for the boys, even for the oldest of those present, seventeen-year-old Melchiorre, whose burgeoning whiskers conferred on him the odd aspect of an actual crew member of the Royal Navy. The conversation, or rather the dialogue between Don Batassano and Ferrara, revolved exclusively around two topics: the price of land in the area surrounding Palermo as compared with the area surrounding Gibilmonte, and anecdotes about aristocratic Palermitan society. Don Batassano considered all these nobles "paupers," even those in possession of a fortune equal to his own, be it only in collections of antiques and leaving income aside. Loath to leave his village, with the exception of rare trips to the provincial capital and even rarer ones to Palermo to "follow" cases in the appellate court, he did not know a single one of these nobles personally and had created an abstract and unvarying image of them, similar to what audiences imagine with respect to Harlequin or Captain Fracasse. Prince A. was a spendthrift, Prince B. a philanderer, Duke C. violent, Baron D. a gambler, Don Giuseppe E. a swordsman, the Marquis F. "aesthetic" (meaning an "aesthete," a euphemism in its turn for worse things), and so on and so forth, each a contemptible picture-card cutout. In these opinions Don Batassano demonstrated a formidable propensity for error, and it can be said there was no epithet that was not erroneously yoked to a name, and certainly no defect that was not fantastically exaggerated, while the real faults of such people remained unknown to him. It was clear that his mind worked in abstractions and that it enjoyed making the purity of the Ibbas stand out against the corrupt background of the old nobility.

Ferrara's knowledge of things was a bit better, but it too was full of gaps, and hence, when he sought to contradict the most outlandish assertions, he quickly ran short of arguments; it was also true that his words provoked such moralistic indignation in Don Batassano that he soon fell silent; in any case they were almost through with dinner.

This had been, in Ferrara's opinion, excellent. The lady Laura was not given, in matters of food, to Pindaric flights; she offered Sicilian cuisine raised to another level —to its cube, in fact—in terms of the number of portions and the abundance of sauces, thus rendering it lethal. The macaroni veritably swam in oil, buried under a mass of caciocavallo cheese; the meats were stuffed with fiery salami; the "trifle in a hurry" contained three times the prescribed amount of liqueur, sugar, and candied fruit. But all this, as previously said, seemed to Ferrara exquisite, the pinnacle of cuisine; on the rare occasions he lunched at Casa Salina, he always came away disappointed by the insipid food. The following day, however, back in Palermo, after having delivered the 78,200 lire to the young prince, Fabrizietto, he described the meal he had been served, and since he knew the prince's fondness for Pré Catelan's *coulis de volaille* and Prunier's *timbales d'écrevisses*, he feigned horror at what he had found excellent; and thus he did something rather pleasing to Salina, who then, during his low-stakes poker game at the club, recounted every detail to his friends, who were always eager for news about the legendary Ibbas; and everyone laughed until the moment when the impassive Peppino San Carlo declared a queens full.

As previously mentioned, curiosity among the noblemen of Palermo with regard to the Ibba family was intense. Curiosity is also the mother of fable, and in these years in fact it gave birth to a hundred fantasies about this sudden fortune. The fantasies testified not only to the childishly ebullient imagination of the upper classes but also to an unconscious discomfort at seeing that it was possible, at the dawn of the twentieth century, to assemble a great fortune based exclusively on land, a form of wealth that each of these gentlemen, from bitter experience, knew to be demolition material, unsuited to the construction of grand edifices. These same property owners felt that the Ibbas' modern reincarnation of the boundless fields of grain of the Chiaromonte or the Ventimiglia of centuries past was irrational and even, for them, dangerous; hence they secretly opposed it, and not only because this imposing structure was in large part erected with material that had previously belonged to them, but because they perceived it as a manifestation of the permanent anachronism that is the brake on the wheels of the Sicilian cart, an anachronism that many perceived but none escaped or avoided supporting in some way.

It bears repeating that this discomfort remained latent in the collective unconscious, only emerging in the guise of tall tales and jokes, as befits a class that makes scarce use of general ideas. The first and most elementary form of such tales is the exaggeration of figures, always elastic in our part of the world. Notwithstanding the ease with which such things might be verified, Batassano Ibba's fortune was appraised at several tens of dozens of millions; one bold individual dared to speak once of "almost a billion" but was silenced, truth be told, because this figure, commonplace today, was so rarely employed in 1901 that nearly everyone was ignorant of its true meaning, and in that time of gold lira coins, to say a billion lire was as much as to say nothing. Concerning the origins of this fortune similar fantasies were woven: The humility of Don Batassano's birth was difficult to exaggerate (old Corrado Finale, whose mother was a Santapau, had hinted that Batassano was the son of a brother-in-law of his who had for a time resided in Gibilmonte, but the tale was given little credence on account of Finale's well-known habit of attributing to himself or his relatives the secret paternity of whatever notorious figure was under discussion, be it a victorious general or celebrated prima donna); on the other hand, the single ordinary corpse that had troubled Don Gaspare was multiplied by ten, by a hundred, and there was no liquidation of an individual occurring in the previous thirty years (and quite a few had occurred) that was not imputed to the Ibbas, who were nevertheless, penally speaking, in fine shape. This was, however surprisingly, the most benevolent aspect of the legend, because the fact of violence, when unpunished, was at the time considered estimable, the halos of Sicilian saints being bloody.

To these locally sown inventions were added the transplants. Dusted off for this purpose, for instance, was the story told a hundred years earlier of Testasecca, of how he had ordered a narrow canal to be dug and his hundreds of cows and thousands of sheep gathered uphill, then milked simultaneously, providing King Ferdinand IV with the spectacle of a brook of frothy warm milk running before him. This fable (not without a certain poetic, specifically pastoral quality, which ought to have betrayed its Theocritean origin), with the simple substitution of Umberto I for King Ferdinand, now came to be charged to Don Batassano. And though it was frightfully easy to prove that the former sovereign had never set foot on the Ibba lands, the tale survived, indisputable.

It was for these reasons for malice mixed with fear that, when the poker game broke up, the conversation turned again to the topic of the Ibbas. A group of ten members had gathered on the club's terrace, which overlooked a peaceful courtyard and was shaded by a tall tree that rained down lilac petals on the mostly elderly gentlemen. Servants in red and blue brought drinks and cups of gelato. From the depths of a wicker armchair came the unfailingly irascible voice of Santa Giulia.

"Honestly, now, can anyone say how much land this wretched Ibba really has?"

"We can, and I do. Thirty-five thousand four hundred acres," San Carlo answered coolly.

"That's all? I thought it was more."

"Thirty-five thousand? Rubbish! According to people who've been there, it can't be less than fifty thousand acres, that's dead certain, and all of it prime farmland."

General Làscari, who appeared immersed in his reading of the *Tribuna*, abruptly lowered the newspaper and showed his liverish face, lined with yellow wrinkles, in which stood out, severe and slightly sinister, the extremely bright whites of the eyes, like those of certain Greek bronzes.

"The figure is seventy thousand acres, not one more and not one less. My nephew, whose cousin is the wife of Ibba's prefect, told me so. That's the way it is, and so be it; there's no point in discussing it further."

Pippo Follonica, a visiting Roman envoy, began to laugh. "Honestly, if you're so interested, why not send someone to look at the cadastral register? It's easy to find out the truth, this truth at least."

The rationality of the proposal was but indifferently received. What Follonica failed to understand was the emotional rather than statistical nature of the discussion: These gentlemen were exchanging envies, grudges, fears, all things that cadastral documents would not suffice to sooth.

The general fumed. "When *I* tell you something, there is no need for cadasters, nor counter-cadasters." His good manners then mellowed him toward the guest. "Dear Prince, you do not know what the cadaster is like in our parts! The transfer deeds are never registered, which means you'll still find individuals listed as owners who have sold everything and moved into the poorhouse."

Confronted with a refutation so rich in local detail, Follonica tried another tack. "Let us concede that the total number of acres remains obscure, but the value of the property in the hands of this boor, who arouses so much passion in you, must be known!"

"This we know very well: eight million net."

"Rubbish!" Thus did every sentence out of Santa Giulia's mouth begin. "Rubbish! Not one cent less than ten!"

"What world are you living in? You don't know anything about anything! He's got twenty-five million in land alone. Then there's the rents, the capital he's loaned out and not yet turned into property, the value of the livestock. That makes at least another fifteen million." The general had laid down his newspaper and was clearly distressed. The imperiousness of his manner had for years been a source of irritation to the entire club—each of whose members wished to be the only one making incontrovertible statements—such that there immediately formed against this opinion a coalition of renewed antipathies and, without reference to the greater or lesser truth of the facts, the appraised value of the Ibba properties fell precipitously.

"This is all fantasy. Claims about money, like those about saintliness, ought to be taken with a grain of salt. If Batassano Ibba has ten million, all included, that's already a lot."

The figure had been distilled from nothing, that is, out of polemical necessity; but when it was spoken, corresponding as it did to the desire of each man, it calmed everyone down, with the exception of the general, who gesticulated from the depths of his armchair, powerless against his nine adversaries.

A waiter entered carrying a long wooden pole, at its tip

a burning bit of spirit-infused flock. The gentle glow of sunset gave way to the harsher light of a gas lamp. The Roman was rather enjoying himself. It was his first time in Sicily, and during his five-day stay in Palermo he'd been received in several houses and begun to change his mind about the supposed provincialism of Palermitan society: the dinners had been well served, the reception rooms beautifully appointed, the ladies elegant and full of grace. But now, this impassioned discussion about the fortune of an individual whom none of the disputants knew nor wished to know, this blatant exaggeration, this hysterical gesticulation over nothing, caused him to reconsider anew. It all reminded him a bit too much of the conversations he would hear in Fondi or in Palestrina, when he went to attend to his estates, and perhaps also of the Bésuquet pharmacy, a memory that, ever since he'd read Daudet's *Tartarin*, never failed to make him smile. And so he laid in a supply of anecdotes to tell his friends a week later when he would be back in Rome. But he was mistaken. He was too much a man of the world to be accustomed to plunging his investigation below the most superficial appearances, and what appeared to him the humorous exhibition of provincialism was anything but comic; it was the tragic convulsions of a class that saw its own primacy as large landowners—that is, its own raison d'être and the source of its social continuity—slipping away, and that sought in arbitrary exaggerations and contrived reductions outlets for its anger, relief for its fears.

Since it was impossible to arrive at the truth, the

conversation strayed. The interlocutors still aimed at an investigation of the private affairs of Batassano Ibba, but set about considering those pertaining more specifically to his person.

"He lives like a monk. Gets up at four in the morning, heads to the piazza to take on the day's workers, looks after his business interests all day long, eats nothing but pasta and vegetables with olive oil, and every night he's in bed by eight."

"A monk married with eight children, mind you," Salina protested. "One of my employees spent twenty-four hours in the man's home. The house is ugly but large and comfortable—decent, in other words. The wife must have been beautiful once. The children are well dressed, actually one is studying here in Palermo. And the food served at his table is heavy but plentiful, as I've already described to you."

The general held firm. "You believe everything people tell you, Salina; or, let's say, they wanted to throw smoke in the eyes of that employee of yours, who must be a fool. Bread, cheese, and oil lamps, that's Ibba's daily life, his true life. It's obvious that when someone arrives from Palermo, he puts on a display to dazzle us, or so he flatters himself."

Santa Giulia writhed in his chair under the impetus of the information he wished to communicate; his well-shod feet stamped the floor, his hands trembled, cigarette ash stippled his jacket. "Gentlemen, gentlemen, you are speaking utter rubbish, and could not be more mistaken.

I know how things stand there. The wife of one of my field wardens is from Torrebella, just down the road from Gibilmonte; every so often she goes to see a sister of hers who married someone there, and she tells her everything. No source more certain than that, it seems to me." He sought confirmation of his own certainty in the eyes of each man, and as everyone was enjoying themselves, he easily found it. Despite the absence of any modest ear to respect, he lowered his voice; without this melodramatic precaution, the effect of the revelations would not have been the same.

"There's a cottage, two and a half miles from Gibilmonte, that Don Batassano had built and fit out in the most luxurious manner you can imagine, with Salci furniture and all the rest." Bits of what he recalled from Catulle Mendès novels, nostalgic reminiscences of Parisian brothels, yearnings long fostered but never fulfilled appeared before his mind's eye. "He called Rochegrosse from Paris to fresco all the rooms; the great painter stayed three months in Gibilmonte and demanded one hundred thousand lire every month." (Rochegrosse had in fact been in Sicily two years earlier: He'd stayed for eight days, along with his wife and three children, and left again after quietly visiting the Cappella Palatina, Segesta, and the quarry prisons in Syracuse.) "It cost a fortune, but what frescoes! Stuff to raise the dead! Nude women, all nude, dancing, drinking, coupling with men and with each other, in every position, in all possible ways. Masterpieces! An encyclopedia, I'm telling you, an encyclopedia of pleasures! Nothing less than what you'd expect from a Parisian given one hundred thousand lire a month and a free hand. Don Batassano received them there by the dozens: Italian women, Frenchwomen, Germans, Spaniards. La Belle Otero was there once as well, of that I'm certain. There an Ibba created his personal Parc aux Daims, like Louis XVI."

This time Santa Giulia had truly made an impression; to a man his listeners sat stunned. Not that they believed him, but they found the fantasy highly poetic; each of them wished for Ibba's millions so that others would invent similarly sumptuous lies about him.

The first to shake off the poetic spell was the general. "And how do you know this? Have you been in the cottage? As an odalisque, or a eunuch?"

Everyone laughed, including Santa Giulia. "I've already told you: My warden Antonio's wife has seen the paintings."

"Excellent! So your warden's a cuckold!"

"Rubbishy rubbish! She was there to drop off some sheets she'd washed. They didn't have her in, but a window was open and she saw everything."

The castle of lies was clearly extremely fragile, but so beautiful—made up of women's thighs, obscene acts without names, great painters, and one 100,000 lire bills—that no one wanted to blow on it and make it fall.

Salina pulled out his watch. "My goodness, it's already eight! I must get home to dress. Tonight is *La Traviata* at the Teatro Politeama, and Bellincioni singing 'Amami, Alfredo!' is not something to be missed. See you in our box."

OTHER NEW YORK REVIEW CLASSICS

For a complete list of titles, visit www.nyrb.com or write to:
Catalog Requests, NYRB, 435 Hudson Street, New York, NY 10014

J.R. ACKERLEY Hindoo Holiday*
J.R. ACKERLEY My Dog Tulip*
J.R. ACKERLEY My Father and Myself*
J.R. ACKERLEY We Think the World of You*
HENRY ADAMS The Jeffersonian Transformation
RENATA ADLER Pitch Dark*
RENATA ADLER Speedboat*
CÉLESTE ALBARET Monsieur Proust
DANTE ALIGHIERI The Inferno
DANTE ALIGHIERI The New Life
KINGSLEY AMIS The Alteration*
KINGSLEY AMIS Girl, 20*
KINGSLEY AMIS The Green Man*
KINGSLEY AMIS Lucky Jim*
KINGSLEY AMIS The Old Devils*
KINGSLEY AMIS One Fat Englishman*
WILLIAM ATTAWAY Blood on the Forge
W.H. AUDEN (EDITOR) The Living Thoughts of Kierkegaard
W.H. AUDEN W.H. Auden's Book of Light Verse
ERICH AUERBACH Dante: Poet of the Secular World
DOROTHY BAKER Cassandra at the Wedding*
DOROTHY BAKER Young Man with a Horn*
J.A. BAKER The Peregrine
S. JOSEPHINE BAKER Fighting for Life*
HONORÉ DE BALZAC The Human Comedy: Selected Stories*
HONORÉ DE BALZAC The Unknown Masterpiece *and* Gambara*
MAX BEERBOHM Seven Men
STEPHEN BENATAR Wish Her Safe at Home*
FRANS G. BENGTSSON The Long Ships*
ALEXANDER BERKMAN Prison Memoirs of an Anarchist
GEORGES BERNANOS Mouchette
ADOLFO BIOY CASARES Asleep in the Sun
ADOLFO BIOY CASARES The Invention of Morel
CAROLINE BLACKWOOD Corrigan*
CAROLINE BLACKWOOD Great Granny Webster*
NICOLAS BOUVIER The Way of the World
MALCOLM BRALY On the Yard*
MILLEN BRAND The Outward Room*
SIR THOMAS BROWNE Religio Medici and Urne-Buriall*
JOHN HORNE BURNS The Gallery
ROBERT BURTON The Anatomy of Melancholy
CAMARA LAYE The Radiance of the King
GIROLAMO CARDANO The Book of My Life
DON CARPENTER Hard Rain Falling*
J.L. CARR A Month in the Country*
BLAISE CENDRARS Moravagine
EILEEN CHANG Love in a Fallen City

* *Also available as an electronic book.*

JOAN CHASE During the Reign of the Queen of Persia*
UPAMANYU CHATTERJEE English, August: An Indian Story
NIRAD C. CHAUDHURI The Autobiography of an Unknown Indian
ANTON CHEKHOV Peasants and Other Stories
GABRIEL CHEVALLIER Fear: A Novel of World War I*
RICHARD COBB Paris and Elsewhere
COLETTE The Pure and the Impure
JOHN COLLIER Fancies and Goodnights
CARLO COLLODI The Adventures of Pinocchio*
IVY COMPTON-BURNETT A House and Its Head
IVY COMPTON-BURNETT Manservant and Maidservant
BARBARA COMYNS The Vet's Daughter
EVAN S. CONNELL The Diary of a Rapist
ALBERT COSSERY The Jokers*
ALBERT COSSERY Proud Beggars*
HAROLD CRUSE The Crisis of the Negro Intellectual
ASTOLPHE DE CUSTINE Letters from Russia*
LORENZO DA PONTE Memoirs
ELIZABETH DAVID A Book of Mediterranean Food
ELIZABETH DAVID Summer Cooking
L.J. DAVIS A Meaningful Life*
VIVANT DENON No Tomorrow/Point de lendemain
MARIA DERMOÛT The Ten Thousand Things
DER NISTER The Family Mashber
TIBOR DÉRY Niki: The Story of a Dog
ARTHUR CONAN DOYLE The Exploits and Adventures of Brigadier Gerard
CHARLES DUFF A Handbook on Hanging
BRUCE DUFFY The World As I Found It*
DAPHNE DU MAURIER Don't Look Now: Stories
ELAINE DUNDY The Dud Avocado*
ELAINE DUNDY The Old Man and Me*
G.B. EDWARDS The Book of Ebenezer Le Page
MARCELLUS EMANTS A Posthumous Confession
EURIPIDES Grief Lessons: Four Plays; translated by Anne Carson
J.G. FARRELL Troubles*
J.G. FARRELL The Siege of Krishnapur*
J.G. FARRELL The Singapore Grip*
ELIZA FAY Original Letters from India
KENNETH FEARING The Big Clock
KENNETH FEARING Clark Gifford's Body
FÉLIX FÉNÉON Novels in Three Lines*
M.I. FINLEY The World of Odysseus
THOMAS FLANAGAN The Year of the French*
EDWIN FRANK (EDITOR) Unknown Masterpieces
MASANOBU FUKUOKA The One-Straw Revolution*
MARC FUMAROLI When the World Spoke French
CARLO EMILIO GADDA That Awful Mess on the Via Merulana
MAVIS GALLANT The Cost of Living: Early and Uncollected Stories*
MAVIS GALLANT Paris Stories*
MAVIS GALLANT Varieties of Exile*
GABRIEL GARCÍA MÁRQUEZ Clandestine in Chile: The Adventures of Miguel Littín
ALAN GARNER Red Shift*

WILLIAM H. GASS On Being Blue: A Philosophical Inquiry*
THÉOPHILE GAUTIER My Fantoms
JEAN GENET Prisoner of Love
ÉLISABETH GILLE The Mirador: Dreamed Memories of Irène Némirovsky by Her Daughter*
JOHN GLASSCO Memoirs of Montparnasse*
P.V. GLOB The Bog People: Iron-Age Man Preserved
NIKOLAI GOGOL Dead Souls*
EDMOND AND JULES DE GONCOURT Pages from the Goncourt Journals
PAUL GOODMAN Growing Up Absurd: Problems of Youth in the Organized Society*
EDWARD GOREY (EDITOR) The Haunted Looking Glass
JEREMIAS GOTTHELF The Black Spider*
A.C. GRAHAM Poems of the Late T'ang
WILLIAM LINDSAY GRESHAM Nightmare Alley*
EMMETT GROGAN Ringolevio: A Life Played for Keeps
VASILY GROSSMAN An Armenian Sketchbook*
VASILY GROSSMAN Everything Flows*
VASILY GROSSMAN Life and Fate*
VASILY GROSSMAN The Road*
OAKLEY HALL Warlock
PATRICK HAMILTON The Slaves of Solitude
PATRICK HAMILTON Twenty Thousand Streets Under the Sky
PETER HANDKE Short Letter, Long Farewell
PETER HANDKE Slow Homecoming
ELIZABETH HARDWICK The New York Stories of Elizabeth Hardwick*
ELIZABETH HARDWICK Seduction and Betrayal*
ELIZABETH HARDWICK Sleepless Nights*
L.P. HARTLEY Eustace and Hilda: A Trilogy*
L.P. HARTLEY The Go-Between*
NATHANIEL HAWTHORNE Twenty Days with Julian & Little Bunny by Papa
ALFRED HAYES In Love*
ALFRED HAYES My Face for the World to See*
PAUL HAZARD The Crisis of the European Mind: 1680–1715*
GILBERT HIGHET Poets in a Landscape
RUSSELL HOBAN Turtle Diary*
JANET HOBHOUSE The Furies
HUGO VON HOFMANNSTHAL The Lord Chandos Letter*
JAMES HOGG The Private Memoirs and Confessions of a Justified Sinner
RICHARD HOLMES Shelley: The Pursuit*
ALISTAIR HORNE A Savage War of Peace: Algeria 1954–1962*
GEOFFREY HOUSEHOLD Rogue Male*
WILLIAM DEAN HOWELLS Indian Summer
BOHUMIL HRABAL Dancing Lessons for the Advanced in Age*
DOROTHY B. HUGHES The Expendable Man*
RICHARD HUGHES A High Wind in Jamaica*
RICHARD HUGHES In Hazard*
RICHARD HUGHES The Fox in the Attic (The Human Predicament, Vol. 1)*
RICHARD HUGHES The Wooden Shepherdess (The Human Predicament, Vol. 2)*
INTIZAR HUSAIN Basti*
MAUDE HUTCHINS Victorine
YASUSHI INOUE Tun-huang*
HENRY JAMES The Ivory Tower
HENRY JAMES The New York Stories of Henry James*

HENRY JAMES The Other House
HENRY JAMES The Outcry
TOVE JANSSON Fair Play *
TOVE JANSSON The Summer Book*
TOVE JANSSON The True Deceiver*
RANDALL JARRELL (EDITOR) Randall Jarrell's Book of Stories
DAVID JONES In Parenthesis
KABIR Songs of Kabir; translated by Arvind Krishna Mehrotra*
FRIGYES KARINTHY A Journey Round My Skull
ERICH KÄSTNER Going to the Dogs: The Story of a Moralist*
HELEN KELLER The World I Live In
YASHAR KEMAL Memed, My Hawk
YASHAR KEMAL They Burn the Thistles
MURRAY KEMPTON Part of Our Time: Some Ruins and Monuments of the Thirties*
RAYMOND KENNEDY Ride a Cockhorse*
DAVID KIDD Peking Story*
ROBERT KIRK The Secret Commonwealth of Elves, Fauns, and Fairies
ARUN KOLATKAR Jejuri
DEZSŐ KOSZTOLÁNYI Skylark*
TÉTÉ-MICHEL KPOMASSIE An African in Greenland
GYULA KRÚDY The Adventures of Sindbad*
GYULA KRÚDY Sunflower*
SIGIZMUND KRZHIZHANOVSKY Autobiography of a Corpse*
SIGIZMUND KRZHIZHANOVSKY The Letter Killers Club*
SIGIZMUND KRZHIZHANOVSKY Memories of the Future
GIUSEPPE TOMASI DI LAMPEDUSA The Professor and the Siren
GERT LEDIG The Stalin Front*
MARGARET LEECH Reveille in Washington: 1860–1865*
PATRICK LEIGH FERMOR Between the Woods and the Water*
PATRICK LEIGH FERMOR Mani: Travels in the Southern Peloponnese*
PATRICK LEIGH FERMOR Roumeli: Travels in Northern Greece*
PATRICK LEIGH FERMOR A Time of Gifts*
PATRICK LEIGH FERMOR A Time to Keep Silence*
PATRICK LEIGH FERMOR The Traveller's Tree*
D.B. WYNDHAM LEWIS AND CHARLES LEE (EDITORS) The Stuffed Owl
SIMON LEYS The Hall of Uselessness: Collected Essays
GEORG CHRISTOPH LICHTENBERG The Waste Books
JAKOV LIND Soul of Wood and Other Stories
H.P. LOVECRAFT AND OTHERS The Colour Out of Space
DWIGHT MACDONALD Masscult and Midcult: Essays Against the American Grain*
NORMAN MAILER Miami and the Siege of Chicago*
CURZIO MALAPARTE Kaputt
CURZIO MALAPARTE The Skin
JANET MALCOLM In the Freud Archives
JEAN-PATRICK MANCHETTE Fatale*
OSIP MANDELSTAM The Selected Poems of Osip Mandelstam
OLIVIA MANNING Fortunes of War: The Balkan Trilogy*
OLIVIA MANNING Fortunes of War: The Levant Trilogy*
OLIVIA MANNING School for Love*
JAMES VANCE MARSHALL Walkabout*
GUY DE MAUPASSANT Afloat
GUY DE MAUPASSANT Alien Hearts*

JAMES MCCOURT Mawrdew Czgowchwz*
WILLIAM MCPHERSON Testing the Current*
DAVID MENDEL Proper Doctoring: A Book for Patients and Their Doctors*
HENRI MICHAUX Miserable Miracle
JESSICA MITFORD Hons and Rebels
JESSICA MITFORD Poison Penmanship*
NANCY MITFORD Frederick the Great*
NANCY MITFORD Madame de Pompadour*
NANCY MITFORD The Sun King*
NANCY MITFORD Voltaire in Love*
MICHEL DE MONTAIGNE Shakespeare's Montaigne; translated by John Florio*
HENRY DE MONTHERLANT Chaos and Night
BRIAN MOORE The Lonely Passion of Judith Hearne*
BRIAN MOORE The Mangan Inheritance*
ALBERTO MORAVIA Boredom*
ALBERTO MORAVIA Contempt*
JAN MORRIS Conundrum*
JAN MORRIS Hav*
PENELOPE MORTIMER The Pumpkin Eater*
ÁLVARO MUTIS The Adventures and Misadventures of Maqroll
L.H. MYERS The Root and the Flower*
NESCIO Amsterdam Stories*
DARCY O'BRIEN A Way of Life, Like Any Other
YURI OLESHA Envy*
IONA AND PETER OPIE The Lore and Language of Schoolchildren
IRIS OWENS After Claude*
RUSSELL PAGE The Education of a Gardener
ALEXANDROS PAPADIAMANTIS The Murderess
BORIS PASTERNAK, MARINA TSVETAYEVA, AND RAINER MARIA RILKE Letters, Summer 1926
CESARE PAVESE The Moon and the Bonfires
CESARE PAVESE The Selected Works of Cesare Pavese
LUIGI PIRANDELLO The Late Mattia Pascal
JOSEP PLA The Gray Notebook
ANDREY PLATONOV The Foundation Pit
ANDREY PLATONOV Happy Moscow
ANDREY PLATONOV Soul and Other Stories
J.F. POWERS Morte d'Urban*
J.F. POWERS The Stories of J.F. Powers*
J.F. POWERS Wheat That Springeth Green*
CHRISTOPHER PRIEST Inverted World*
BOLESŁAW PRUS The Doll*
QIU MIAOJIN Last Words from Montmartre*
RAYMOND QUENEAU We Always Treat Women Too Well
RAYMOND QUENEAU Witch Grass
RAYMOND RADIGUET Count d'Orgel's Ball
FRIEDRICH RECK Diary of a Man in Despair*
JULES RENARD Nature Stories*
JEAN RENOIR Renoir, My Father
GREGOR VON REZZORI An Ermine in Czernopol*
GREGOR VON REZZORI Memoirs of an Anti-Semite*
GREGOR VON REZZORI The Snows of Yesteryear: Portraits for an Autobiography*
TIM ROBINSON Stones of Aran: Labyrinth

TIM ROBINSON Stones of Aran: Pilgrimage
MILTON ROKEACH The Three Christs of Ypsilanti*
FR. ROLFE Hadrian the Seventh
GILLIAN ROSE Love's Work
WILLIAM ROUGHEAD Classic Crimes
CONSTANCE ROURKE American Humor: A Study of the National Character
SAKI The Unrest-Cure and Other Stories; illustrated by Edward Gorey
TAYEB SALIH Season of Migration to the North
TAYEB SALIH The Wedding of Zein*
JEAN-PAUL SARTRE We Have Only This Life to Live: Selected Essays. 1939–1975
GERSHOM SCHOLEM Walter Benjamin: The Story of a Friendship*
DANIEL PAUL SCHREBER Memoirs of My Nervous Illness
JAMES SCHUYLER Alfred and Guinevere
JAMES SCHUYLER What's for Dinner?*
SIMONE SCHWARZ-BART The Bridge of Beyond*
LEONARDO SCIASCIA The Day of the Owl
LEONARDO SCIASCIA Equal Danger
LEONARDO SCIASCIA The Moro Affair
LEONARDO SCIASCIA To Each His Own
LEONARDO SCIASCIA The Wine-Dark Sea
VICTOR SEGALEN René Leys*
ANNA SEGHERS Transit*
PHILIPE-PAUL DE SÉGUR Defeat: Napoleon's Russian Campaign
GILBERT SELDES The Stammering Century*
VICTOR SERGE The Case of Comrade Tulayev*
VICTOR SERGE Conquered City*
VICTOR SERGE Memoirs of a Revolutionary
VICTOR SERGE Unforgiving Years
SHCHEDRIN The Golovlyov Family
ROBERT SHECKLEY The Store of the Worlds: The Stories of Robert Sheckley*
GEORGES SIMENON Act of Passion*
GEORGES SIMENON Dirty Snow*
GEORGES SIMENON The Engagement
GEORGES SIMENON Monsieur Monde Vanishes*
GEORGES SIMENON Pedigree*
GEORGES SIMENON Red Lights
GEORGES SIMENON The Strangers in the House
GEORGES SIMENON Three Bedrooms in Manhattan*
GEORGES SIMENON Tropic Moon*
GEORGES SIMENON The Widow*
CHARLES SIMIC Dime-Store Alchemy: The Art of Joseph Cornell
MAY SINCLAIR Mary Olivier: A Life*
TESS SLESINGER The Unpossessed: A Novel of the Thirties*
VLADIMIR SOROKIN Ice Trilogy*
VLADIMIR SOROKIN The Queue
NATSUME SŌSEKI The Gate*
DAVID STACTON The Judges of the Secret Court*
JEAN STAFFORD The Mountain Lion
CHRISTINA STEAD Letty Fox: Her Luck
GEORGE R. STEWART Names on the Land
STENDHAL The Life of Henry Brulard
ADALBERT STIFTER Rock Crystal

THEODOR STORM The Rider on the White Horse
JEAN STROUSE Alice James: A Biography*
HOWARD STURGIS Belchamber
ITALO SVEVO As a Man Grows Older
HARVEY SWADOS Nights in the Gardens of Brooklyn
A.J.A. SYMONS The Quest for Corvo
ELIZABETH TAYLOR Angel*
ELIZABETH TAYLOR A Game of Hide and Seek*
HENRY DAVID THOREAU The Journal: 1837–1861*
TATYANA TOLSTAYA The Slynx
TATYANA TOLSTAYA White Walls: Collected Stories
EDWARD JOHN TRELAWNY Records of Shelley, Byron, and the Author
LIONEL TRILLING The Liberal Imagination*
LIONEL TRILLING The Middle of the Journey*
THOMAS TRYON The Other*
IVAN TURGENEV Virgin Soil
JULES VALLÈS The Child
RAMÓN DEL VALLE-INCLÁN Tyrant Banderas*
MARK VAN DOREN Shakespeare
CARL VAN VECHTEN The Tiger in the House
ELIZABETH VON ARNIM The Enchanted April*
EDWARD LEWIS WALLANT The Tenants of Moonbloom
ROBERT WALSER Berlin Stories*
ROBERT WALSER Jakob von Gunten
ROBERT WALSER A Schoolboy's Diary and Other Stories*
REX WARNER Men and Gods
SYLVIA TOWNSEND WARNER Lolly Willowes*
SYLVIA TOWNSEND WARNER Mr. Fortune*
SYLVIA TOWNSEND WARNER Summer Will Show*
ALEKSANDER WAT My Century*
C.V. WEDGWOOD The Thirty Years War
SIMONE WEIL AND RACHEL BESPALOFF War and the Iliad
GLENWAY WESCOTT Apartment in Athens*
GLENWAY WESCOTT The Pilgrim Hawk*
REBECCA WEST The Fountain Overflows
EDITH WHARTON The New York Stories of Edith Wharton*
PATRICK WHITE Riders in the Chariot
T.H. WHITE The Goshawk*
JOHN WILLIAMS Butcher's Crossing*
JOHN WILLIAMS Stoner*
ANGUS WILSON Anglo-Saxon Attitudes
EDMUND WILSON Memoirs of Hecate County
RUDOLF AND MARGARET WITTKOWER Born Under Saturn
GEOFFREY WOLFF Black Sun*
FRANCIS WYNDHAM The Complete Fiction
JOHN WYNDHAM The Chrysalids
STEFAN ZWEIG Beware of Pity*
STEFAN ZWEIG Chess Story*
STEFAN ZWEIG Confusion *
STEFAN ZWEIG Journey Into the Past*
STEFAN ZWEIG The Post-Office Girl*